DARK MOON
Legacy

VOLUME I

The CURSE

CYNTHIA BLAIR

HarperPaperbacks
A Division of HarperCollins*Publishers*

This is a work of fiction. The characters, incidents, and dialogues are products of the author's imagination and are not to be construed as real. Any resemblance to actual events or persons, living or dead, is entirely coincidental.

HarperPaperbacks   *A Division of* HarperCollins*Publishers*
10 East 53rd Street, New York, N.Y. 10022

Produced by Daniel Weiss Associates, Inc.,
33 West 17th Street, New York, New York 10011.

First printing: October, 1993

Printed in the United States of America

HarperPaperbacks and colophon are trademarks of HarperCollins*Publishers*

10 9 8 7 6 5 4 3 2 1

VOLUME I

The CURSE

DuMain, France

THE YEAR

1545

The boy sat alone in the forest, trembling. All around him the shadows deepened, black shapeless forms moving slowly over the dense growth as night smothered day. He started at every sound: the rustling of leaves, the terrible cry of some small creature caught in the talons of an owl, the dull tread of animals' footsteps stealing across the rocky terrain.

Tears were streaming down Pierre Gautier's muddy face onto his clothes, the tattered garments of a shepherd. Completely alone, he had no family, no friends. At eleven years old he had been thrown into the world to fend for himself. There was no one to take care of him, no one to care for him.

And now this. Another sheep gone. Killed

by one of the bloodthirsty wolves that roamed this part of France. Silently they stalked their victims, seeming to strike from out of nowhere. The struggle was one-sided. It took only seconds for the powerful jaws of the wolf to close around the throat of a sheep, crushing bone and flesh between the razor-sharp teeth that gleamed in the pale moonlight. This night hunter showed no mercy. It pounced, it ravaged, it bounded away, disappearing into the dark as silently as it had come.

One more sheep. The third in only a month. Pierre knew that the farmer he worked for would beat him, just as he always did. The mere thought caused a fresh stream of tears to run down his face. Already he could feel the pain of the whip lashing against his flesh.

Somebody help me! he thought, frantic.

He was contemplating running away, desperately clinging to the idea that escape might really be possible, when he heard the thundering. The noise was so loud and so horrific that he clamped his hands over his ears. Yet it wasn't thunder. It came not from above, but from below. The earth itself seemed to shudder.

And then they stood before him. Three

dark horsemen, clothed in black, astride sleek black steeds that towered above him. Wide-eyed, he stared. Never had he seen such magnificent animals. Never had he seen such travelers. Large muscular figures, their shoulders broad beneath dark cloaks, their faces nearly shrouded by hoods.

"Renounce your faith." It was the horseman in the center who had spoken, his voice low and rasping. In the moonlight Pierre saw that his eyes were not eyes at all, but dark circles that burned like coals. Terrified, he looked away.

The horseman went on. His voice was lower now, almost a whisper. "Renounce your faith. Embrace a new lord, and we will protect you."

A terrible fear rushed up inside Pierre, so intense that it was unlike anything he had ever experienced before. Yet it quickly faded. Instead, a feeling of acceptance, of relief, washed over him. It rendered him powerless, banishing any will of his own. His mind was drained of all thought; there was only the feeling of being swept away, carried along by currents too strong to resist.

And then, without realizing he was speaking, he heard his own voice say, "Yes."

After they had gone, he saw that the rocks on which the horses had stood had twelve holes burned into them, one where each of the animals' hooves had been. From their depths rose billows of putrid black smoke.

CHAPTER
1

Miranda Campbell took a deep breath, filling her lungs with crisp autumn air as she rode furiously. Her muscles taut, she used every ounce of her strength to push her bicycle up one of the steeper hills separating her house from Overlook High School.

I can't wait to tell Bobby, she thought, smiling. *He'd better be at his locker.*

She reached the top of the hill, then sailed down the curving incline on the other side. She luxuriated in the feeling of the cool wind whipping her curls around, unconcerned that the mane of wild black hair streaming behind her was probably becoming a crazed tangle. On a perfect October morning like this, when the air was fresh and cool and the leaves were tipped with fiery red and orange, who could be bothered with worrying about anything that unimportant?

Then, as she rounded the bend, an unexpectedly icy gust of wind momentarily held her in its grip, a harbinger of the approaching winter.

Miranda glided downward so fast she was just on the edge of being out of control, rushing past the tall cedars that covered the green Oregon foothills running along the craggy coast. Just beyond, the proud and powerful Cascade Mountains dwarfed everything around them. On the other side were the crushing waves of the Pacific Ocean, breaking against rocks so sharp and so treacherous that this section of the beach had been nicknamed Devil's End. Thick white curls of mist rose off the sea, turning the small sleepy town into a magical place.

As Miranda rounded another sharp curve, she started. A wolf's head suddenly jutted out of the dense fog. A two-hundred-year-old totem pole loomed above the center of town, covered with the flattened likenesses of animals that had once roamed freely here on the Oregon coast. It was topped by a carving of the most fearsome beast of all, a wolf with its teeth bared and its jaws pulled back into a vicious snarl. She'd seen it a thousand times before. Even so, whenever she happened upon it, it unnerved her a little.

In the fifth grade, Miranda had written a report on the totem pole, hoping that understanding its origins might loosen its mystical grip on her. It was Overlook's most familiar landmark, a piece of Native American history that the town's residents took pride in. She'd learned a lot about the tribe that had once occupied this spot, living off both land and sea, recording its genealogy on intricately carved totems like this one. Yet even now, the totem pole caused her to gasp involuntarily. Quickly she looked away.

She turned a corner and found herself at the edge of the schoolyard. Instead of sliding across the smooth asphalt of paved roads, she now bumped over rocky dirt and scraggly grass. Her schoolbooks, tossed carelessly into the wicker bicycle basket, were jostled about. Straight ahead was the low brick school building. The morning mist was so thick she could barely see it. To her left was the football field, and to her right, the edge of the dense woods that crept up the hills. The forest was a presence here, as it was everywhere else in Overlook.

Miranda veered off toward the bike rack. Now that she was almost there, she was more eager than ever to find Bobby. This exuberant feeling was something she couldn't wait to share.

She lifted her books out of her bicycle basket. Her math textbook, a thick stack of spiral notebooks . . . and a library book, a well-worn copy of *Wuthering Heights* by Emily Brontë. She adored reading novels, particularly romantic ones, with strong, courageous heroines like Brontë's Cathy.

Miranda headed toward the wide doors of the school. The corridors of Overlook High were crowded. Students stood together in clumps, chattering and gossiping against a backdrop of beige metal lockers. Some were already hurrying off to homeroom. Bulletin boards dotted the walls, colorful collages of notices and newspaper clippings and posters.

Miranda walked along, pushing strands of unruly dark hair out of her eyes.

"Hi!" she called again and again as she passed people she knew from her classes as well as from the clubs and committees she was always joining.

She craned her neck as she neared the end of the main hall, where Bobby's locker was. The two of them met there nearly every morning before school. She usually found him surrounded by his friends, who scattered when she appeared. Becoming a varsity basketball player had catapulted Bobby McCann from the role of an easygoing guy whom nearly everybody liked to a real star. These days he was always in the center of things, up there with Miranda in the ranks of the school's best known and most popular seniors.

Sure enough, there he was, hanging out with Kevin Burke, a gawky redheaded boy, and tall, wiry Ricky Garcia. Kevin and Ricky were both on the team.

"Bobby!" Miranda said impatiently. "I've got to talk to you."

Kevin and Ricky exchanged glances as Bobby and Miranda kissed each other hello.

"Uh-oh," Ricky teased. "Better leave these two alone. C'mon, Kev. We're outta here."

Bobby was wearing the wide, lopsided grin that reduced half the girls at Overlook High to jelly. "Okay. So what's up?"

"Bobby, the most fantastic, wonderful, amazing, incredible thing in the entire universe has just happened—"

"Whoa! Slow down!"

"Okay. Have you ever heard of the Pacific Players?"

"Let me guess. They put on plays, right?"

"Right. They're considered one of the best community theater groups in all of Oregon."

"And . . . ?"

"Bobby, you're not going to believe this! Last night I got a telephone call from Ms. James. She said the Pacific Players' director called her. He's putting on *Saint Joan*, and since Joan of Arc is seventeen when the action takes place, he wants a high school girl to play the lead. He invited Ms. James to pick some girls to try out!"

Bobby broke into his famous grin again. "And of course Miranda Campbell, actress *extraordinaire*, was the first name that came to mind."

"Well, I was one of her choices, anyway." Miranda was blushing.

"Way to go, Miranda!" Suddenly he frowned. "Wait a minute. Now that you're on the verge of becoming a star, does that mean you don't want to be seen with a commoner like me anymore?"

Miranda brushed aside his teasing question. Anxious to get through an awkward moment, she cooed melodramatically, "Oh,

Robert, you'll always be my leading man."

Seriously she added, "I haven't actually gotten the part yet."

"Oh, you'll get what you want. You always do."

Before Miranda had a chance to respond, Bobby said, "I suppose you had Corinne and Selina on the phone eight seconds after you heard."

"Believe it or not, you're the first to know—aside from my parents."

"I bet they're excited."

"Well, sure."

Actually, they'd seemed distracted when Miranda had told them, as if they had something else on their minds. That seemed to be the case more and more lately.

"So who else is trying out?" Bobby asked. "Anybody you know?"

"I have a few ideas. Some of the girls in my theater-arts class are pretty good—"

"Not as good as you," Bobby insisted.

He bent down and gave her another kiss, this one much longer and slower.

Miranda closed her eyes and leaned her head against his shoulder, luxuriating in the feeling that from now on, everything was going to be just fine.

*   *   *

Miranda had only a minute or two before the bell rang, but she had to stop by the chemistry lab to tell her two closest friends, Corinne Davis and Selina Lamont, the good news.

When she turned the corner she spotted Selina lingering outside the classroom, studying the bulletin board.

"Selina!"

She was petite, with short dark-brown hair and soft, pretty features. Most outstanding were her large green eyes, at the moment assessing an oversize poster advertising the upcoming spring dance. Selina, known around school for her passion for bright colors, was dressed in a neon-pink T-shirt and multicolored tie-dye stretch pants.

She barely glanced up. "Oh, hi, Miranda. Listen, check out this poster for the Homecoming Dance next week. Pretty cool, huh? It was my idea to use lime-green cardboard—" She happened to glance over her shoulder then, and she stopped midsentence.

"What's with you? You look like you just won the lottery."

Miranda laughed. "Better. I've got some great news. Where's Corinne?"

"She's out sick. I stopped at her house on my way to school, and her mother told me she was in bed with a sore throat."

"Poor Corinne!"

Selina grimaced. "I have a feeling her disease is related more to the chemistry quiz than some killer virus. So tell me!"

"I've been invited to audition for the Pacific Players!"

"The theater group?"

Miranda nodded. "They're putting on *Saint Joan* and the director wants a high school girl to play the lead."

"Awesome!" Selina made no attempt to hide how impressed she was. "Good going, Miranda! Only seventeen and already on your way to stardom."

"Not quite," Miranda assured her, laughing. "But it's bound to be fun. And it's an honor just to be picked for the audition."

"I'll say. So what did the love of your life have to say?"

Miranda's smile suddenly felt forced. "Bobby's pretty excited."

"Excited enough to forget about last weekend?"

Miranda found herself regretting having confided in Selina about what had happened

Saturday night. She realized now she'd have been better off pouring her heart out to her diary.

She thought back to the weekend before. She and Bobby had parked on a quiet street after a party at Corinne's. Miranda loved kissing Bobby. The softness of his lips, the warmth of his body . . . a wonderful sweetness flowed through her as she shut out the rest of the world, concentrating only on him.

"This is so nice," Miranda had sighed, nestling her head against his shoulder.

"It could be even nicer," Bobby replied.

Instantly Miranda tensed. This wasn't the first time this issue had come up. And just like the other times, it caused a wall to spring up between them.

"Come on, Miranda," Bobby said impatiently. "You know I really care about you. Besides, we're not kids anymore."

"I know. But—"

"I thought you loved me."

"I do. It's just that . . ."

She let her voice trail off. She did care about Bobby. And part of her did want to take their relationship to a more intense level. Yet something was holding her back.

"I'm just not ready, Bobby," she'd insisted.

His voice had had a hard edge to it as he'd said, "If you're not ready by now, when are you going to be?"

She'd stared out the car window, not wanting to look at him. "Maybe never."

Bobby drove her home and kissed her good night tenderly, if briefly, and neither of them had mentioned the argument again. Still, a strain lingered between them. It was suddenly clear that they viewed their relationship differently. She kept wishing things could simply go back to the way they'd been before.

Now she tried to shrug off Selina's question. "So we had a little fight. All couples do," she insisted.

"Sure they do."

Miranda wished Selina sounded more convincing. "So when's the audition?"

"Next Wednesday."

"So *soon*?"

Miranda grimaced. "For the next week I'll be eating, breathing, and sleeping Joan of Arc. Ms. James said it's a really demanding role—"

Just then the bell went off, its shrill ring causing Miranda to jump.

"Relax, Miranda. You'll do fine. But I've

got a date with a Bunsen burner. Not as glamorous as a life in the theater, maybe, but I'd take a passing grade in chemistry over stardom any day. Catch you later!"

Selina wasn't the only one who was going to be late. Miranda hoped Mr. Wexler would be willing to forgive an aspiring actress for dashing into English class a few seconds after the bell.

"Mo-o-m? Where are you?" Miranda dropped her books onto the table in the front hall. Usually there was a bouquet of fresh flowers in its center, carefully arranged in a graceful crystal vase. Today, she noticed, there was none.

"I'm in the kitchen!"

"Mom, I just had a great idea. How would you feel about helping me memorize my lines for the—"

Miranda stopped in her tracks the moment she entered the kitchen. Not only was her mother standing there, gripping the counter; her father was also home. Usually he was out of the house until at least seven or eight, his Jeep careening across the curving, sometimes treacherous back roads of this untamed section of Oregon. Dr. Campbell was the local veterinarian, and it was a job that consumed almost all his time.

Yet there he was. Clearly something was very wrong.

"Mom? Dad?" Miranda felt the color draining out of her face. "Is everything all right?"

"Honey, sit down," her mother said without looking her daughter in the eye.

"What's wrong? Is somebody sick?"

"No, nothing like that." Her mother sat down next to her at the table. Gently she took her hand, offering a weak smile. "We've been waiting for the best time to tell you, and, well, we finally realized that there really isn't any such thing as a best time." She took a deep breath. "Miranda, your father and I have decided to live apart for a while. It's just a trial separation, a way for us to see if perhaps we can—"

"What?" Miranda pulled her hand away. "What are you talking about?"

"Sweetie, I'll still see you as often as before," her father insisted, his voice strained. "Maybe I'll even see you more. I've rented a house over in Norton. It's only a couple of miles away. You can get there on your bike or I could pick you up in the Jeep—"

"No!" Miranda was on her feet. She felt dizzy, as if everything were suddenly whirling around out of control.

"Honey, it's just a trial separation," her mother said softly. "It's not as if—"

"You can't do this! You're my parents. You're supposed to love each other!"

Her mother and father exchanged helpless glances. Miranda realized then that all the signs had been there—the arguments late at night, the silences the next morning, the tension that hung in the air as thick and as stifling as smoke. The warnings had been there—she just hadn't wanted to see them. And now it was all too clear how much both of her parents were hurting.

She wanted to comfort them, but her own pain was too great. Miranda raced out of the house. The sun had disappeared behind a cloud and the air had grown chilly. But she couldn't go back for a jacket. She grabbed her bike and climbed on, determined to ride as fast as she could.

But as Miranda pedaled, the dizzy feeling that had first enveloped her in the kitchen grew. Blindly she rode, having no idea where she was going, knowing only that she had to get away.

She went west, heading for the foothills, where the inclines were excruciatingly steep. Miranda was pushing herself much too hard, she knew, but the physical pain of exertion was better than mentally replaying the devastating scene she'd just witnessed.

Finally, at the top of a hill, she dropped her bike, unable to go on. The muscles in her legs cramped, her chest heaved, and she could no longer hold back the violent sobs that racked her entire body.

"No!" she cried, knowing there was no one to hear. "Please, please, don't let this be happening! Please, no!"

When she finally opened her eyes, burning from the salt of her tears, she caught sight of the totem pole and started. The snarling wolf at its pinnacle appeared to be staring at her, the late-afternoon light turning its evil eyes smug.

Miranda shuddered and lowered her eyes.

She climbed back on her bike. What had started out as a day in which it seemed nothing could go wrong had suddenly become the worst day of her entire life. Soon she was again pedaling as hard as she could, putting everything she had into trying to block out the pain.

CHAPTER
2

As Miranda rode her bicycle to school through the mist the next morning, she was shrouded in sadness. A cold wind whipped off the coast, bearing down on her and making it nearly impossible to scale the steeper hills. Despite her energetic riding, she moved along in slow motion, overwhelmed by the formidable wind.

She was exhausted; her brain was coated with cobwebs. She'd spent a long night tossing and turning, wishing desperately for the release sleep would bring. But the luxury of rest eluded her.

Hour after hour she'd lain in the dark, the red numbers on her digital clock taunting her. Two o'clock, three o'clock, four o'clock . . . she watched the numbers change, trying to let them hypnotize her into sleep. Instead she saw her mother's face, then her father's, both of them tensed, pained, and fearful. Accompanying these images was an empty, lonely feeling, lodged so firmly in the pit of her stomach that she wondered whether it would ever go away.

Now she just wanted to be alone. Yet as she neared the schoolyard, she saw Corinne and Selina in front of the bike rack, waiting for her.

"Hi," she called with forced gaiety. She'd already decided that she wasn't ready to start telling people about her parents—not even her closest friends. The shock was still too great for her to even imagine saying the words.

"Hi, Miranda." Selina looked her usual whimsical self, dressed in an oversize orange sweater over a black miniskirt. But Miranda thought she detected a strain in her voice.

Corinne, too, seemed strange. Her blue eyes were cold, ironically making her striking beauty even more pronounced. Corinne Davis looked like a model. Tall and thin, her hair was a glossy gold, her skin impossibly creamy, her cheekbones well-defined.

Corinne and Miranda had been friends

for over a decade. They'd met in the first grade, where they were rivals for the role of teacher's pet. As they grew older, their competitiveness continued, spurring them on, with each blithely trying to top the other.

Once they reached high school, however, Miranda began to sense there was occasionally an edge to their sparring. While Corinne was easily the prettiest girl at school, she'd never been as well-liked as Miranda. A lot of people at Overlook High thought Corinne was conceited—more self-absorbed than she ought to be, Miranda knew. And while Miranda was always the first to rush to Corinne's defense, she understood how people could have formed that opinion.

"You know, Miranda," Corinne said, not bothering to say hello as was often her habit. "You and I have known each other for a long time. When two people have been friends for so many years, sooner or later something like this is bound to come up."

"Something like what? What are you talking about?"

Her first thought was her parents: *How on earth had Corinne and Selina found out already?*

Selina glanced at Corinne. "She hasn't heard."

"Heard what?"

"We're talking about the play," said Corinne. "*Saint Joan.*"

A wave of relief swept over Miranda. She wouldn't have to talk about her parents' separation just yet. "What about it?"

"Miranda," Selina said softly, casting her eyes downward, "you're not the only one who was invited to audition for the lead."

"I know. Ms. James said—"

"Did you know Corinne was also chosen?"

Miranda broke into a wide smile. "That's fantastic! Congratulations, Corinne!"

Corinne wasn't smiling. As for Selina, her eyes were still cast on the gravel at her feet.

"I really want this part," said Corinne.

Miranda was struck by the intensity of her tone. "I think everyone who's trying out really wants it." She glanced from Corinne to Selina. "It's a chance of a lifetime."

"I'm sure you're right. I'm sure every single girl who was asked to audition is dying for the part." Corinne paused, twirling a strand of her long golden hair around her finger. "But I intend to get it."

"Maybe you should drop out, Miranda,"

Selina suggested, her tone only half joking. "You know, spare yourself the humiliation of losing."

Corinne laughed. "Maybe that's not such a bad idea."

The bell rang. Selina glanced nervously toward the door. "We'd better get going."

Miranda didn't move. She stood looking at Corinne, not quite believing what was happening. "Getting that part's important to me, too, Corinne," she said in a soft voice. "I also want it."

"Well, then, I guess we're in for an exciting competition." Corinne turned toward the school, then glanced back over her shoulder, offering an icy smile. "May the best woman win."

He watched her from the woods, shielded by the dense growth of trees. Peering through the branches, he saw the entire scene unfold before him as if he were watching a play. With his sensitive ears he heard their voices. He saw how hurt she was. And he felt her sorrow as if it were his own.

Miranda, they called her.

He didn't know her. He'd never even seen her before. Yet something about her intrigued him.

When the girl with the golden hair—the one who pretended to be her friend—had spoken to her so coldly, he had flinched. He watched as Miranda tensed her muscles, bracing herself. Yet still she carried her tall, slender frame with dignity, with pride. Only he, it seemed, could see the shock in her eyes. The heaviness of her shoulders. The subtle firmness at the corners of her mouth.

He knew all about pain.

It wasn't until she'd raised her face to the sun peeking out of the morning mist for the first time that day, that he'd seen her beauty. The thick, dark tangle of hair, curling around her soft features. The slender nose, the full lips. Her eyes, as dark as the earth after a rain, shone with tears she would not let fall.

Yet there was something else about her, something that seemed to emanate from within. As if her physical beauty were a reflection of what was inside. He sensed that she possessed a goodness that few others had. A deep strength, as well, and the courage to fight for what she knew to be right. After the others had gone, he watched her stand in the schoolyard. She'd barely moved, still proud, still strong, despite the hurt inflicted by their words.

How he longed to go to her! To grab her

shoulders, to pull her against him, to tell her
that he knew. That he understood. And that
something in him longed to make it all right.

He felt such a powerful pull toward her,
unlike any feeling he had ever experienced
before. It surprised him. It *frightened* him. To
feel such a connection, so quickly, so irra-
tionally. This attraction, he knew, could well
have the power to control him. To make him
let go of all his resolve . . . to forget the
promises he had made to himself in his most
rational moments.

To feel what he was determined never to
feel.

That possibility was the most terrifying of
all.

After homeroom, Miranda made her way
through the crowded corridor in a fog. The
faces of the other students and the colors of
their clothes mixed and passed by her like
the swirls of a kaleidoscope. The conversa-
tions and the laughter jumbled together, fading into the background, nothing more than
a meaningless din. It was like being in a fun
house—except that she wasn't having any
fun.

And then, all of a sudden, she collided

with something. Gasping, she looked up and saw it was another girl.

"Oh, I'm sorry!" Miranda cried, embarrassed.

"It's okay. No problem." Elinor Clay, a student in Miranda's theater class, looked a little dazed. She brushed her chin-length brown hair out of her face and offered a shy smile. She and Miranda had spoken a few times, usually about class assignments. She was a quiet girl, hovering on the edge, not really part of any crowd at school.

"Actually, now that we've—um—bumped into each other," said Elinor with a laugh, "I can tell you how much I loved your reading from *A Midsummer Night's Dream.* You did a terrific job."

"Thanks. Your monologue was good, too."

"Broadway, here we come," Elinor said teasingly. "Speaking of which, I heard you've been picked to audition for *Saint Joan.*"

"That's right."

"Congratulations. I've been thinking about getting involved with the Pacific Players, too. Backstage, though. I've decided to go for assistant stage manager."

"Maybe we'll end up working together."

"That'd be great. Not that it'd leave either

of us much time for anything resembling a life—"

The clang of the bell cut their conversation short.

"Well, duty calls." Elinor rolled her eyes. "See you around!"

Miranda watched as Elinor dashed off to her next class, then hurried off to her own.

Sitting in English, waiting for Mr. Wexler to get started, Miranda opened her notebook only to find herself confronted with a page filled with math formulas. She wondered how she was supposed to focus on school with everything that was happening. First her parents, then Corinne and Selina . . .

All of a sudden someone tripped over her foot, jostling her desk and sending her books flying. When she looked up she was face-to-face with Andy Swensen's sneer.

"Ouch!" he cried. "You tripped me."

"Maybe you should watch where you're going," she countered, struggling to keep her tone even.

"Ooooh. Guess I'd better watch out. If I step out of line, Miranda might sic the basketball star on me."

Miranda opened her mouth to reply, then snapped it shut. What was the use? Andy

Swensen had been this way since elementary school. He'd probably spent half his life in the principal's office. The other half he spent annoying people. So instead of protesting, Miranda simply shrugged, then started picking up her books. She had enough to worry about without getting into an argument with the class idiot. But when Mr. Wexler cleared his throat and folded his arms across his chest, she realized it wasn't going to be that easy.

"Mr. Swensen," Mr. Wexler said coldly, "I think you owe Miranda an apology."

"Hey, it wasn't my fault." Andy had already taken his seat on the other side of the room, slumping down in his chair.

"Didn't you hear me?" said Mr. Wexler. "I said apologize."

"It's all right, really," Miranda said. "I don't—"

"Mr. Swensen, I'm going to tell you one more time."

By this point, every pair of eyes in the room was fixed on Andy. Usually he enjoyed being the center of attention. Today, however, he looked angry. Embarrassed, too. He tended to pick on other guys, goading them into fighting. Miranda was hardly his usual prey.

"All right, all right." Andy rolled his eyes

upward. "Sor-ry, Mi-ran-da."

Some of the girls tittered. One of Andy's pals, Dave Falco, reached over and slapped him on the back. Miranda was relieved when Mr. Wexler went over to the blackboard after casting one more glare in Andy's direction.

"All right, let's get started." With dramatic strokes he wrote on the board: Research Project.

"Now that your senior year is underway, you're going to be tackling something a little more rigorous than what you're used to," he said, peering at the class from under his thick dark eyebrows. "It's time for you to get to know one of my best friends: Will Shake-speare."

The class let out a collective groan. Miranda, listlessly opening her English note-book, didn't participate. Somehow, com-pared to everything else she had to deal with, a research paper on the works of William Shakespeare was the last thing in the world worth groaning about.

Miranda took the long way home, opting to walk through the woods. Wheeling her bike over the bumpy terrain was awkward, but she didn't care. She longed for the peace she knew being in the forest would bring. Getting through an entire day at school, pretending she was fine, had been a strain. She hadn't even told Bobby about her parents. She'd tried when she saw him at lunch, but the words just wouldn't come.

Miranda walked slowly. This was one day she was in no hurry to get home. Her father was moving his things out, something she'd rather not have to see.

Her spirits lifted the moment she found herself in the midst of the towering cedars and full pines, inhaling the damp air of the forest and revelling in its familiar sounds. Being in the presence of nature left untamed always helped her put things in perspective. It reminded her that she was just a tiny part of the earth, inconsequential in the larger scheme of things.

By the time she emerged from the woods, her shoes muddied but her spirits considerably higher, the sun was getting low in the sky. She hesitated outside her house, standing in the backyard, bracing herself before going in. And then Miranda noticed something on the back porch.

Walking closer, she saw it was a bouquet of wildflowers, tied together with a scrap of pink satin ribbon. As she gently picked up the burst of colorful blossoms, she caught sight of a piece of paper tucked among the leaves.

"For Miranda," she read aloud. Underneath was a poem. It was written in ink in a hand she didn't recognize, the cursive letters neat and rounded as if they had been formed with painstaking care.

> *The tears that fill your sad dark eyes*
> *Are like the dew at dawn's new day:*
> *They make the flowers' beauty shine*
> *Then quickly, mercifully hasten away.*

There was no signature, no way of knowing who'd written it. Bobby had never done anything like this before; besides, this wasn't his handwriting. Miranda glanced around, feeling her cheeks grow warm. She half expected the mysterious poet to be standing in the yard. But she was alone, surrounded only by stillness.

She folded the piece of paper and tucked it safely into her pocket. Then she buried her face in the soft petals of the wildflowers, closing her eyes as she inhaled their sweet fragrance.

CHAPTER
3

As Miranda joined the throng of students making their way through the corridors of Overlook High the next morning, she wore in her hair a yellow wildflower, its delicate petals just beginning to droop. She was basking in the same dreamy mood that had come over her the afternoon before. She wore it like a cloak, wrapped around her, keeping her safe and snug, helping to ward off the sadness that threatened to engulf her totally. What a welcome distraction it was.

She couldn't stop thinking about her secret admirer. Who was he? How had he known what she was going through . . . and why had he cared?

She also debated whether or not she should mention it to Bobby. The idea of keeping something from him was peculiar. They had known each other for so long it would have been hard to say when they'd progressed from being "just friends" to becoming boyfriend and girlfriend. They'd grown up together. As children they spent long days playing together. They'd picked marionberries, gathered shells on the white sand, roamed the lush green hills that surrounded Overlook in search of Native American artifacts.

But in ninth grade everything changed. It happened in the spring, at the first real dance she'd ever been to. Miranda had come with Selina and Corinne. When they both ran off to reapply their lipstick in the bathroom, she gravitated toward Bobby, relieved to find someone familiar.

When they'd decided to slow-dance together, it had been in the spirit of experimentation. But being so close to Bobby, touching him, feeling his breath on her cheek . . . by the time Miranda went home that night, everything had changed. All of a sudden her childhood pal had become someone who was special in a whole new way.

Those first few months, she felt more alive than she'd ever felt before. Being in love was exhilarating, a feeling of being swept up onto a higher plane. All she wanted was to be with Bobby. Eating, sleeping, and doing homework were nothing more than bothersome intrusions.

Eventually that first rush of excitement passed. Their relationship evolved into something more comfortable. They didn't quite take each other for granted, but they both knew there would be few surprises. They each got more involved in interests of their own. Bobby spent most of his time playing basketball. The fact that he'd grown nine inches between his thirteenth birthday and his fourteenth, placing him well above the six-foot mark, made him one of the strongest players on the school's team. She, meanwhile, indulged more and more in her love of books and plays and movies, luxuriating in the all-absorbing stories of characters who led lives filled with romance, passion, and danger.

By now Miranda Campbell and Bobby McCann were an institution at Overlook High. Every once in a while, though, she found herself wondering what had happened to the excitement, the romance, the feeling that anything might happen. But then she'd reason that reliability and security

were more important than romance any day.
Right now that seemed more valid than ever.

In the end, she decided not to mention
the bouquet and the poem to Bobby. He
might feel threatened, and the last thing she
wanted to do was risk starting another argument. Besides, she'd decided she was ready to
tell him about her parents. She needed to tell
him. The evening before had been excruciating. She'd holed up in her room, unable to
concentrate on reading or studying or even
flipping through a magazine. Through her
closed door, she could hear her father pack-
ing his things and making countless trips to
load up his Jeep.

An oppressive silence had hovered in
the house. Miranda had felt so alone . . .
and so frightened. She longed for someone
to lean on. It was then she knew it was time
to tell Bobby. She almost called him, but
then decided it wasn't something she could
discuss over the telephone. She had to tell
him in person. She even found herself
looking forward to it, hoping that talking
about it with somebody she could trust,
somebody who would understand what she
was going through, would make it hurt a little less.

She was about to turn down the corridor where his locker was when Elinor Clay fell into step beside her.

"How's it going, Miranda?" she asked as they snaked their way through the chattering students rushing off to their lockers or their classrooms.

Miranda sighed. "Between Mr. Wexler's Shakespeare paper and the trials of Joan of Arc, this is going to be one busy semester."

"You'll manage," Elinor assured her. "By the way, I found out I've got some competition too. Turns out I'm not the only one interested in being assistant stage manager. Still, I'm hoping for the best—"

Miranda's attention suddenly shifted. There was a commotion near Bobby's locker. A girl was shrieking, her sharp voice cutting through the din in the hallway.

"Stop! I can hardly breathe! Oooh, I'm going to get you for this!"

Miranda stood frozen as the scene came into focus. When the girl wasn't screaming, she was laughing. Her long blond hair was whipping around wildly. Somebody, a boy, was tickling her without mercy.

Her name was Amy Patterson. She was the girlfriend of Bobby's teammate Kevin, so she

and Miranda had struck up a casual friendship, sitting together on the bleachers during the games, cheering on their boyfriends.
Still, she wasn't really Miranda's type. Amy
tended to laugh too loudly, meanwhile keeping an eye out to make sure other people
were noticing her.

Like now. She was doubled over, acting as
if being tickled in the ribs was the most hilar-
ious thing that had ever happened to her.
Miranda's heart stopped as she realized that
the boy who was tickling Amy wasn't Kevin. It
was Bobby.

Miranda stood perfectly still as she
watched. Neither Bobby nor Amy had noticed her. She saw Elinor glance over at her,
gauging her reaction, then hurry off to
class.

Calling upon every ounce of control she
possessed, Miranda walked over and tapped
Bobby on the shoulder. "Excuse me," she
said calmly, "but I think that girl needs some
oxygen."

Bobby looked up at her and turned
bright red. Miranda saw his hazel eyes were
filled with guilt.

"Miranda." He swallowed hard.

Beside him, Amy stood up, assessed the

situation, and gave a toss of her head. "Why, *hello* there," she said, her words syrupy. "I didn't know you showed up at school this early."

"So I gather." Miranda cast her a hard look, then did an instant replay for Bobby's benefit. "I hope I didn't interrupt anything."

Amy laughed shrilly. "Oh, we were just playing around." Her eyes were fixed on Miranda's as she gave Bobby a light jab in the arm. "This guy knows all the right spots."

"Yes, doesn't he?" Miranda's eyes were fixed on the girl, daring her to continue.

Amy shook her head so that her blond locks shimmered, and looked at Bobby coyly. "I guess it's time for me to check out. Catch you later, Bobby."

Miranda watched as, with a little wave, Amy disappeared into the crowd.

"What was that all about?" Miranda asked, trying to keep her voice light.

"Oh, nothing. We were just messing around." Bobby had turned to his locker, where he was busily shuffling books around. "You know how Amy is."

"I do now." Miranda bit her lip. She didn't want to get into this right now.

"Bobby, I really need to talk to you."

"Yeah? What is it? Anything wrong?" As he turned toward her, Miranda could tell he was doing his best to look interested. He wore the look that meant he was really focusing on her. Usually that look made her feel warm inside, as if the two of them really did have a special connection. Today, however, she found herself mistrusting it.

"I . . . today . . . look, maybe we can get together during lunch and talk. What I have to tell you about is not exactly the kind of thing I feel like discussing in the middle of the hallway."

"Okay. Let's meet at the bleachers at the beginning of fifth period." Bobby was looking at her in a strange way. "Miranda, are you all right?"

She looked down, blinking hard. At the moment, she wasn't sure what the answer to that question was.

Miranda sat on the edge of a bleacher seat at the football field, mindlessly bending the corner of a notebook back and forth. The yogurt she'd bought in the cafeteria sat on the bench next to her, untouched. The wildflower, by now wilted, was tucked between the pages of a book, momentarily forgotten. Miranda was nervous about meeting Bobby. She tried to tell herself it was because of what she was preparing to tell him about her parents, but she knew it wasn't just that.

The scene with Amy Patterson had prompted an unsettling wave of self-doubt and fear. She tried to convince herself that Bobby's tickling Amy Patterson was harmless. Even so, as Miranda replayed the argument she'd had with Bobby a few days earlier, she feared that it was anything but.

The knot in her stomach tightened when she saw him jogging across the schoolyard, waving.

"Hi." He was breathless as he sank onto the seat beside her. "Sorry I'm late."

"You're not late." Was it only her imagination or was he having a hard time looking her in the eye?

Bobby exhaled sharply, trying to catch his breath. "So what's up?"

Miranda smiled. Walking here through the schoolyard, she'd rehearsed the exact words she wanted to say. She'd planned to sound calm, rational . . . matter-of-fact, even. Instead, she burst into tears.

"Bobby, my parents are splitting up!"

"Oh, no." He reached over and took her hand in his. "Tell me everything."

She spilled out the story of her parents' announcement. As she spoke, her tears gradually dried and her sobs grew less frequent. It was a relief to tell him, she realized, just as she'd hoped. He did, after all, know her almost as well as she knew herself. Suddenly she didn't feel quite so alone.

He waited a moment after she stopped talking, carefully considering her words. "It may just be a temporary thing," he said finally. "It sounds as if your parents are going through a tough time right now. Maybe being apart for a while is the best way for them to work out whatever problems they're having."

"Do you think so?" That was the one possibility she'd been clinging to. It made her feel better to hear someone else voice it.

"Yes," he said, smiling and touching her cheek, "I think so. And Miranda, if there's anything I can do . . ." Bobby's voice trailed off uncertainly as he withdrew his hand. "Well, you know that you can count on me."

"Thanks," she said, nodding, her voice nearly a whisper.

An unspoken question still hovered between them, creating an awkward silence. It was Bobby who broke it. "I guess this is as good a time as any to talk about this morning."

She just looked at him. Part of her longed to brush the incident with Amy aside, to tell him he didn't have to answer to her. But another part was burning with the recollection of what she'd seen that morning. And that part wanted an explanation.

"Amy and I were just clowning around. I know it probably *looked* bad, but—" His cheeks were bright red. "Amy and Kevin just broke up and—"

"They did?" The words burst out.

"Yeah. Just yesterday. Anyway, I was only trying to make her feel better."

"Well, I think you did a terrific job." Miranda immediately bit her lip. She hadn't meant to sound mad, but the anger was still there; she couldn't deny it. She was hurting, and so far Bobby had done nothing to help make the hurt go away. "I had such an awful feeling when I saw the two of you together this morning."

"Put your 'awful feeling' away." He took her hand again, this time bringing it up to his lips and kissing it gently. "It's you I love,

Miranda. I could never be interested in anybody else. You know that."

As she looked into his pleading eyes, she
almost believed him.

He had been standing there for a long
time, shielded by the trees surrounding the
schoolyard. Watching. Waiting.

The first time he'd seen her, it had been
by accident. This time he had sought her
out.

Ever since the day before, he hadn't
stopped thinking about her. She was in every
vibrant wildflower he saw. In every breath of
fresh air he sucked hungrily into his lungs.
In the sweet songs of the birds of the forest,
their clear voices rising up from the stillness.

He wanted to see her again. To know she
was safe. To revel in her presence.

And so he stayed in the woods near the
school, hoping for even a glimpse of her.
The seconds moved slowly, the sounds of the
forest his only company.

And then his heart began to pump wildly.
Someone was coming. There, in the distance, moving toward him.

Was it Miranda?

The figure grew nearer, and he knew.

Already so much about her was familiar to him. Her tall, slender silhouette. The halo of untamed black hair that she pushed away distractedly. And above all the proud way in which she carried herself, as if to say that nothing, no one, could defeat her.

He moved closer as she settled into the bleachers alongside the football field. From where he now stood, he could see her face. His heart pounded so loudly he feared she would hear it.

But she took no notice. He could tell she was not aware of anything around her. She was hidden behind the barriers she had put up to keep herself safe. He knew all about that.

And so he watched, unseen. He saw the boy come, the one she called Bobby. He heard them talking. He heard the boy's empty promises, his meaningless reassurances. He heard her replies, filled with hope even as her uncertainty grew.

And then after the boy had gone, leaving her alone, he once again saw tears glistening in her dark brown eyes, drops of sadness gathering there to spill down her soft cheeks.

Her shoulders began to shake. His heart ached when she buried her face in her hands. She was letting the tears come, giving in to them, unable or unwilling to hold them back. Seeing her cry made him feel as if some evil thing had reached into his chest and clamped its gnarled fingers around his heart.

His lips formed one word. "Miranda."

He longed to show himself. To emerge from his hiding place in the woods, to tell her . . . tell her what? The terrible secret that kept him from her? Reveal the thing that held him apart from all the others, that dragged him through this tormented existence, day after day after day? That, he knew, was impossible.

Still, he had to reach out to her. The power she had over him was impossible to resist. It was like a kind of magic, pulling him toward her, despite logic, despite reason.

Despite fear.

He would touch her life again. Already the words were forming in his mind. Words meant to comfort her, to ease her pain, to tell her she was not alone.

Words meant to touch her in a way he knew his yearning flesh never could.

When Miranda spotted the folded piece of paper in her bicycle basket—yellow, this time, the same color as the wildflower she'd been wearing in her hair—she knew what it was right away. Eagerly she grabbed it, not even bothering to look around. Even if he were watching her, she knew he wouldn't reveal himself. Instead, she scanned the handwritten lines.

> *When darkness like a cloud descends*
> *And banishes the light,*
> *When day is just a memory*
> *And all there is is night,*
> *When heaviness engulfs your heart,*
> *Crushing it like a stone,*
> *Find hope in knowing, through it all,*
> *That you are not alone.*

She felt herself begin to smile warmly just when the piece of paper was jerked out of her hand.

"What—"

She turned and saw Andy Swensen, wearing a triumphant grin as he dashed off, her poem in his hand. At his side were two of his thuggish friends, Dave Falco and Mark O'Neill.

"Give me that!" she demanded, refusing to give him the pleasure of running after him.

"Hey, guys, check this out!" Andy taunted.

"Maybe I got only a C in English, but I know a love poem when I see one."

"Read it out loud!" Mark demanded.

"With pleasure."

"Andy, grow up!" Miranda tried to grab the poem, but Andy's sidekicks got in her way.

In the same singsong voice in which he'd made his halfhearted apology, he began to read. "'When dark-ness like a cloud descends—'"

"Andy," Miranda cried, "if you don't give that back, I'll—"

"You'll what?" he challenged. "Sic the poet on me? Oooh, I'm scared, I'm really scared."

He laughed a grating laugh, then continued reading aloud. "'When day is just a mem-o-ry and all there is is night—'"

Miranda cringed as the mocking voice pronounced the beautiful, sensitive words of the poem. She felt her face turning red, her hands clenching into tight fists. Part of her wanted to run. Yet she wanted the poem back. It was hers.

Andy continued. "Hey, get this. 'When heav-i-ness engulfs your heart, crushing it like a sto-o-one, find hope in knowing, through it all, that you are not a-lo-o-one.' Nice rhyme scheme."

"Are you finished?" Miranda demanded,

pushing her way past Mark and Dave and holding out her hand.

"Take it. I never did like poetry." He tossed it onto the ground. Letting out one more loud hoot, he turned and stomped off, taking his idiot pals with him.

Once they were gone, Miranda snatched the paper off the ground. She was so angry she was shaking. *How dare he,* she thought. *Someone like Andy, who's simply not capable of understanding . . .*

As she glanced down at the piece of paper, the last line caught her eye.

"'Find hope in knowing, through it all, that you are not alone,'" she read aloud.

The thought gave her comfort—even though she had no idea who had written those words. It helped her just to know he was out there, thinking of her. That someone knew what she was going through. Someone who felt what she felt, who understood her pain. Someone who *cared.*

If only she knew who he was.

CHAPTER 4

As Miranda rode away from school toward the Overlook library, she forced herself to think about *Romeo and Juliet*. She desperately needed a distraction, and she'd decided that holing up at the library for the afternoon to work on her English project was as good a diversion as any.

She'd decided to write about *Romeo and Juliet* because suddenly, everything she thought she knew about love was up for grabs. Perhaps by studying two of literature's most famous lovers, she'd stop feeling as if the boy-girl thing were a game that everyone else knew the rules to—except her.

As it was, everything was crumbling before her eyes: her parents' twenty-year marriage, her relationship with Bobby, even her friendship with Corinne and Selina. The things that had always seemed as solid and reliable as the imposing Cascade Mountains she'd grown up with were now shaky and uncertain. Even the sudden appearance of her anonymous poet was confusing.

As she turned onto the main street of Overlook, she headed toward the grocery store to grab something quick to eat before delving into her Shakespeare.

The Overlook Grocery always made Miranda feel as if she had taken a step back in time. She pushed against the wooden screen door with its peeling dark green paint and was greeted by the tinkling of the bell hung overhead. Inside, there were uneven wooden floors and shelves packed with everything from cornflakes to laundry soap to cans of soup. Hanging down from the ceiling were large straw baskets and giant metal pots and pans. The air was fragrant with cinnamon, ground coffee, and fresh bread baked in the kitchen at the back of the store.

"Afternoon, Miranda." The grocery store's proprietor, Mr. Henry, wiped his hands on his white apron. "What can I get for you today?"

"Hi, Mr. Henry. Just an apple, please."

"They're in back, like always. Help yourself."

Bushel baskets piled high with fresh produce lined the far wall of the long, narrow store. As she made her way through the aisles at the back, she saw two women from town.

"Look at this. Soft spots. Honestly, you'd think Mr. Henry could get some decent vegetables in every once in a while." Virginia Swensen, Andy's mother, shook her head as she tossed a cucumber back into the basket.

Her friend, Margaret Donahue, shook her head. "I guess we have no choice but to drive to the Safeway in Norton."

Be our guest, Miranda thought in defense of the store she'd loved since childhood. *We certainly wouldn't miss you here.* Andy's mother and her friend Mrs. Donahue were the town gossips and it was typical of them to stand around complaining about produce whenever they weren't spreading rumors. Still, Miranda nodded a hello in their direction, then looked over the shiny apples piled high in their bins. She was trying to decide between a Cortland and a Mac when the bell on the door tinkled its welcome once again.

Miranda glanced up and saw that a small

woman hunched with age had come into the store. She had a wise face, one that reminded Miranda of a crab-apple doll with its weathered skin, sharp features, and black, piercing eyes. No one knew exactly how old Feather-Woman was. Some people said she was a hundred years old. Others claimed she was even older, so old that she'd actually been part of the tribe of Native Americans who populated the Oregon coast back before the white settlers had come.

"Isn't this a nice surprise!" Mr. Henry's face lit up. "What can I get for you today, FeatherWoman?"

Mrs. Swensen, not bothering to lower her voice, said, "She probably needs some herbs for one of her magic potions."

"Careful, Virginia," her friend replied. "You don't want to get scalped."

"That's not fair!" Miranda spat out the words before she could stop them. She'd turned to face the two women, her dark eyes ablaze with fury.

Mrs. Donahue looked shocked. Then, with a knowing nod of her head, she turned to her friend and whispered something behind her hand.

Miranda stormed to the front of the store.

FeatherWoman was standing at the counter, waiting patiently as Mr. Henry weighed a mound of herbal tea leaves.

"Hello, FeatherWoman," said Miranda, placing her apple on the counter. "I don't know if you remember me. My name is Miranda Campbell, and—"

"I know who you are." The old woman reached over and placed her wrinkled hand on Miranda's arm. "You came to me many years ago to learn about my people."

"That's right!"

FeatherWoman's face clouded, and suddenly she seemed to be talking more to herself than to Miranda. "The totem, with its many dark, dark secrets. And now there will be trouble. There's change in the air."

"Change?" Miranda repeated.

"There is a terrible restlessness among the narnauks."

The narnauks. Miranda tried to remember what FeatherWoman had taught her about the narnauks. They were the spirits the tribes of the Pacific Northwest believed in. Evil spirits, but good spirits as well. They could be found everywhere in nature, and were very much a part of Native American life. It was even possible to communicate with them, mostly through dreams and trances, but also through physical meetings.

Slowly FeatherWoman's words dawned on her.

"A restlessness?" she repeated. "What does it mean?"

"A terrible restlessness." The old woman shook her head. "There's going to be—"

"Here you go, FeatherWoman," Mr. Henry said brightly, holding a brown paper bag out to her. "Half a pound of chamomile tea. What else can I get for you?"

Just then Mrs. Swensen and Mrs. Donahue made their way toward the door, walking side by side so that both Miranda and Feather-Woman had to move out of their way. As Virginia Swensen went by, she muttered, "Narnauks indeed!"

Miranda glanced at FeatherWoman, expecting her leathery face to register anger. Instead, the older woman's steely gaze followed Virginia Swensen out the door. Something in those jet-black eyes sent a shiver down Miranda's spine.

The public library had become a sanctuary for him. As he sat surrounded by the dark wood paneling, the thick carpeting, the tall shelves filled with books, he felt protected. The library's heavy, forestlike stillness comforted him. Here, he could be alone. Safe. Undisturbed.

How peaceful it was—not only in the library, but in all of Overlook, he thought, staring without seeing the words of the book that lay open on the table in front of him. How restful, compared to Portland.

Yet more than fleeing from the city itself, he had run away to escape the private torment that had haunted him there. He had done something terrible in Portland, committed an act he could not reverse. All that remained for him now was to try to live with the horror of it . . . and to try to understand.

And so he had fled, coming to Overlook to escape. Here, no one knew him. He could hide, keeping himself separate. Making no friends, taking no risks . . .

His cheeks burned as his thoughts turned to the girl. Miranda. Already he had broken the promise he'd made to himself. He'd taken a risk, sending her those poems. Yet he'd been unable to resist. He felt something for her he had never felt before.

He knew he had to maintain control, to keep a distance between them.

He would have to be careful.

He could manage, he assured himself. He could keep his feelings in check for as long as he stayed in Overlook. This was where he had to be. His roots were here. His family dated back to this area hundreds of years, before there was even a town, back to the time the fur trappers had first come to the New World from France, anxious to seek their fortunes. It was the best place to carry out his mission.

Here, he hoped to find an answer.

Somehow he had to learn. He had to understand. He was living under a curse, something so horrible he could never tell a soul. He had a sense of the strength of the power that controlled him.

He also had a sense that it was evil, so base and so horrific that it was unlike anything else on earth.

He had much to do. He turned back to the heavy tome before him, clinging to the hope that if he could only understand, perhaps he could undo it.

Chaining her bicycle to a pole, Miranda noted that the parking lot of the Overlook Public Library was nearly deserted. That was hardly a surprise; with autumn well underway and winter just around the corner, there wouldn't be many more crisp, sunny days like this one. There weren't bound to be many people willing to spend such an afternoon indoors. Still, she reflected as she pulled on the heavy wooden door, that was fine with her. Solitude and escape were precisely what she was seeking.

As she stepped inside, she instantly left behind all her worldly concerns. The library was a magical place, with its dark walls, thick rugs that silenced every footstep, and long rows of wooden tables with their ornately carved legs. She loved the musty smell of the old books with their tattered covers and dry yellowed pages that sometimes crumbled at the corners when they were turned.

It was in this cavernous room that, as a little girl, Miranda had first discovered the wonders of reading. Amazing worlds had opened up for her, worlds in which animals could talk, fairies and elves were real, and little girls like her could go off on wonderful, wild adventures. The library never failed to restore in her the hope and innocence of her childhood, the belief that anything was possible.

I could use a dose of that about now, Miranda

thought. With a sigh, she headed for the card catalogue.

It didn't take her long to find the call numbers she needed. She jotted down the numbers on the front cover of her spiral notebook, then headed for the open stacks.

"Romeo, Romeo . . ."

Miranda ran her finger along a shelf. As she did, she happened to glance through the bookshelf. It was then she noticed him, sitting at a library table. An open book lay in front of him, but he was staring off, his thoughts clearly somewhere else.

What struck her first was his face. Reflected there was great concentration, a pensive frown that tensed the muscles of his forehead. Even so, she could see he was extremely handsome. He had golden hair, thick and wavy and just a tiny bit unruly. Blond eyebrows topped the bluest eyes she had ever seen. His complexion was light, his nose straight, his chin strong and square. Even though he was lost in thought, there was a sweetness in his expression, as if not all of the boy in him had been lost to the man who was just beginning to emerge.

His physique was similarly remarkable. Although he didn't look much older than she was, he was built like a man, with wide shoulders, well-defined arms, and a powerful chest. The fabric of his shirt, blue-and-white striped cotton, was pulled taut, so strained that it looked as if it might give way to the solid muscles underneath.

Staring at him, Miranda experienced an almost overwhelming desire to run her fingers through his golden curls. Instead, she reached for her own hair, pushing the wavy strands away from her eyes.

Earth to Miranda, she chided herself, snapping back to the task that had brought her here in the first place. As she resumed her search, however, she found her heart was racing. Finally she located *The Complete Works of William Shakespeare*—right where it was supposed to be. But not only was it a tremendous volume, undoubtedly too heavy for her to lift without straining, it was also on the topmost shelf, just beyond her reach.

"Darn!" she said aloud, her frustration reflected in her tone.

"May I help you?"

Surprised, she peeked through the books to see the boy rising from his seat, a shy, tentative smile on his face.

She could feel her cheeks turning pink.

"It's just that the book I need is a little too big and a little too high up."

"Here. Let me get it."

"That's okay," she answered, too quickly. "I'll ask the librarian to help me."

"Which book is it?"

He was already at her side. He was wearing faded jeans, the washed-out denim pulled tightly over his thighs. He was tall, she could see, easily over six feet. Standing this close to him, Miranda was having difficulty catching her breath. Her skin was tingling, and her heart insisted upon pounding even more wildly than before.

"It's that one," she said, trying to keep her tone even.

"William Shakespeare, hmmm?" With ease the boy reached up and took the massive book down from the shelf. "Here you go."

His blue eyes were bright and alive and his face practically glowed as he held out the thick volume. Miranda took a step backward, overwhelmed by how drawn she was to him. It was almost as if a spell had been cast over her. Never before had she had such a strong reaction to anyone.

"It's very heavy," he said. "Can you manage? Or should I put it down somewhere?"

"Uh, anywhere would be fine."

As she followed him back to the table where he'd been sitting, Miranda was struck by how agile he was. Unlike most of the guys she knew, including Bobby, he emanated a sort of grace. He seemed at ease with his body in a way that was not at all typical of guys his age. As he placed the book on the table, she also noticed how large and how strong his hands were.

"Thanks." Miranda sat down, not opening the book.

"You're welcome," he said, still standing.

She was suddenly desperate to find more to talk to him about, to make him stay. "Uh, do you live in Overlook? I don't remember seeing you before."

He stopped for a moment, then said, "I'm from Portland."

"What brings you down here?" Miranda said, surprising herself with her boldness.

Her question caused him to fix his eyes on the corner of the table. "I graduated from high school last spring." He swallowed hard, still refusing to meet her gaze. "Now I'm taking some time off to decide what I want to do next."

Trying to ease his obvious discomfort, Miranda nodded toward the book in front of him. "So I guess that's not homework you're doing."

"No." He hesitated. "I'm doing research. For myself. Actually," he went on, snapping the book closed before she'd had a chance to see what it was, "I'm just about finished. For today, anyway." Abruptly he grabbed the gray suede jacket hanging on the back of his chair.

She wondered if she'd asked too many questions. Still, she couldn't just let him disappear, so she found herself searching for something else to say.

"Overlook must seem quiet, after Portland."

"I like it much better down here," he replied. "I'm not much for city life. I prefer being surrounded by the beauty of the land and the majesty of the sea."

Miranda laughed. "Hanging out at the library must be having an effect on you. You sound like something out of a book!"

She instantly saw that what she'd meant as a compliment caused his face to turn bright red. His blue eyes clouded up.

"Oh, I'm sorry! I only meant—"

"That's okay." Already he was turning away, now distant and cold. "It was nice to meet you."

Miranda's heart sank. *But we didn't really*

meet. And now he was already striding toward
the door. As she watched him walk away, she
felt an emptiness, a kind of sorrow over having been left behind with only a pair of ficti-
tious lovers for company.

"I hope you don't mind eating in here
tonight." Miranda's mother placed two plates
of microwaved macaroni and cheese on the
kitchen table, then sat down opposite
Miranda. As she did, she barely glanced at
her daughter or her food.

"It's fine, Mom. It's kind of cozy, in fact."
Miranda looked down at her plate, thinking
about how it was neither. Missing were the little niceties that had customarily been part of
the Campbells' dinner ritual: a pretty table-
cloth, linen napkins, often a bouquet of flowers or a candle in the center of the table. And
of course, they usually ate dinner in the din-
ing room. Dinner had always been a time for
Miranda and her parents to catch up on one
another's news and to share the events of the
day. A time to be a family.

Tonight, however, was different. Miranda's
father wasn't there, and his absence created an
odd, uncomfortable atmosphere in the house.

Miranda picked up her fork, wondering if

she'd ever get used to this new way of doing things. And eating dinner in the kitchen, she knew, was only the beginning.

"How was school today?" her mother asked with forced cheerfulness. "Anything interesting happen?"

Miranda thought of the boy she'd met after school at the library. But she doubted that, tonight especially, her mother would be interested. Instead, she said, "Actually, I went to the library and started working on this big research project for English. We have to write a paper on one of Shakespeare's plays."

"Which did you choose?" Her mother actually looked interested.

"*Romeo and Juliet.* It's a wonderful play. Still, between writing this paper and memorizing my lines for the audition, I'm really going to have my hands full."

"Have you started learning your part yet?"

Miranda nodded. "I put some time in right before dinner. It's fun, but it's going to be a lot of work."

"You'll manage," her mother said. "You've always been good at the things that were important to you."

"Actually," Miranda confided, glad for the opportunity to talk to her mother like this,

"I'm a little nervous. The Pacific Players are really serious and, well, it's sort of intimidating."

Miranda's mother got up from the table and said distractedly, "You know what they say about spreading your wings."

Miranda toyed with her unfinished dinner, aware that a heavy silence had fallen over the room.

"Mom," she said slowly, keeping her eyes fixed on her plate, "if I get that part, would both you and Dad come watch me?"

As her mother glanced up, a pained look crossed her face.

"Oh, Miranda! Neither of us would ever miss something like that! Your father and I will always be there for you, no matter what happens."

She came over, wrapping her arms around Miranda.

"Oh, Mom, I'm so scared!" Miranda cried, letting the tears flow. "I feel like my whole world is falling apart!"

"I know, I know." Mrs. Campbell gripped her daughter's shoulders. "It's hard for all of us. But we'll get through it. I know we will."

Miranda simply clung to her, holding on as if she had no intention of ever letting go.

Yet even as she did, she knew that the days when her mother could protect her had ended long before.

It was difficult for Miranda to believe she was actually nervous about dropping in on Selina. Yet, as she stood outside her house early that evening, she was apprehensive.

The two girls had been friends for as long as Miranda could remember. She and Selina and Corinne had shared so much over the decade they'd known each other that it was hard for Miranda to sort her past out from theirs. In addition to being in school together all their lives, they'd shared each and every birthday. They'd gone trick-or-treating and Christmas caroling every year, always returning to one of their houses afterward to compare their loot or warm up with hot chocolate. Every time Miranda received a bit of good news, every time something bad happened to her, every time she had a crush on a boy or got an A on a test or came home from a family vacation, it was Corinne and Selina with whom she'd spend hours on the telephone, poring over every single detail.

And now this. This terrible rift. It was bad enough that Corinne was suddenly seeing

Miranda as a rival. That, at least, she could understand, since there was something at stake for both girls. But the way that Selina had chosen sides . . .

Miranda had been fighting feelings of betrayal ever since the confrontation in the schoolyard. She decided she simply had to tackle them headon. As difficult as it was going to be to face Selina, she knew it was the only chance she had to salvage their friendship—a friendship that, at the moment, was on very shaky ground.

Her stomach was in knots as she rang the Lamonts' doorbell. When Selina answered, a look of shock crossed her face.

"Miranda!"

"Are you busy?"

"No, I was just about to do my homework. Of course, I'm always looking for an excuse not to." She laughed, but there was something guarded about her manner. "Come on in."

Miranda had been to Selina's house so many times it was like her second home, but today she felt out of place. She stood awkwardly in the front hall.

"Want to go up to my room?" Selina asked.

"Sure." Upstairs, Miranda perched on the edge of the bed. She glanced around, pretending to be interested in things she'd seen thousands of times before: the pink and green flowered curtains; the photographs of Selina's favorite actors and rock stars, cut out of magazines and tacked on the wall; the collection of dolls sitting on wooden shelves, staring out like the members of a particularly attentive audience.

"Selina," she began, deciding to get to the point, "there's a reason I came by. I want to talk to you about something."

"Okay." Selina's voice was soft, her eyes cast downward.

"Maybe you already know." Miranda took a deep breath. "I was really upset by what happened yesterday. I—I keep hoping I simply misunderstood."

Selina looked at her, her green eyes wide. "Misunderstood what, Miranda?"

"I don't think you and Corinne meant to hurt me. I'm sure you thought you were just being a good friend to her. That all you were doing was supporting her in something that she thinks is important—"

"Look, Miranda, we've been friends for a long time. All three of us. We know each other pretty well. Surely you know Corinne has always been a little bit envious of you."

Miranda winced. "But why, Selina? Friends shouldn't be envious of each other!"

"They should be if one of them always seems to get whatever she wants." She shrugged. "Now *Corinne* wants the role of Joan of Arc. I don't think that's unreasonable."

"Of course it's not unreasonable. And I wish her the best. What I don't understand is why she doesn't wish me the best too."

"You don't?" Selina cast her an odd look. "Why is it so unusual that Corinne wants something for herself?"

Miranda's frustration was growing. "You're twisting my words. I think it's great that she's getting serious about acting. She's good. She stole the show last year in the school play. Everybody said so. She's a strong contender for the lead in *Saint Joan*."

"So what's your point, Miranda?" Selina asked coldly.

"It's simple. I don't want this silly play to get in the way of our friendship. I don't want Corinne holding the fact that she and I were both invited to audition against me. And I certainly don't want you choosing sides. We're *friends*, Selina. All three of us."

"If you're so worried about our friendship, Miranda, how about stepping aside? Why not do what you can to improve Corinne's chances of getting the part?"

Miranda just stared at her. She remained silent for a long time. When she finally spoke, her voice was low and controlled.

"I don't know which hurts more—the way you've decided that you have to take sides, or the way you refuse to see how betrayed I feel."

"I'm sorry." Selina's apology didn't sound the least bit convincing. "But I don't think you understand how much you're hurting Corinne. She really wants this part. For once in her life—for once in *our* lives, Miranda—*she* wants to be the star."

Miranda stood up. "Well, I guess there's nothing left to say. Maybe you and I can simply agree to disagree on this, Selina."

The other girl shrugged. "I suppose." She was pretending to be absorbed in her doll collection.

Before leaving, Miranda turned around one last time. "I know this is turning out to be a tough time, Selina. I'm not sure why, but it is. But there's one thing I want you to know."

Selina glanced up, cocking her head. "What's that?"

"That our friendship is important to me. And that when the auditions are far in the past and the run of the play is finished, I'm not going to let this episode get in our way. We can get past this, Selina, all three of us. We can put it aside and not let it get in our way. I know we can."

"I hope you're right."

There was a hollowness to Selina's words that continued to haunt Miranda even as she let herself out of the Lamonts' house, heading out into what had become a brisk October night.

CHAPTER
5

Miranda and her father had made plans to spend part of the weekend together. She was anxious to see the house he'd rented, wanting to assure herself that he was comfortable in his new place. He picked her up in his Jeep first thing Saturday morning. It was odd, having him pull up in front of the house and honk, rather than coming in. She dashed out, calling good-bye to her mother, who sat at the dining-room table, her face buried in a magazine.

As the two of them drove the few miles to Norton, she told her father all about the events of the week. She knew she was repeating much of what she'd already told him over the phone during their nightly calls, but she wanted to fill the silence she was afraid would fall if she stopped her cheerful chatter.

The house was small, but clean and bright. Wandering from room to room was kind of an adventure. Eagerly she listened to her father talk about his plans for a storage cabinet here, a fresh paint job there. Still, through it all she was plagued by a terrible sadness. When he offered to drive her back right after lunch, she was relieved.

Instead of going home after he'd dropped her off in front of the house, Miranda headed for the woods.

Just as she'd hoped, simply stepping inside the cool, dark enclave caused a welcome peacefulness to descend upon her. Tromping through the underbrush, feeling soft ground and sharp stones through her sneakers, breathing in the damp, sweet air, had a magical way of making her problems seem far, far away. She needed to be here, she realized. Being in the woods like this, all alone and away from everything that was familiar, had a way of replenishing her dispirited soul.

She found herself thinking about her meeting with FeatherWoman. The old woman had spoken of the spirits who lived in nature, the narnauks. In the store, the very notion had seemed like a colorful bit of folk-lore. Here, however, she could understand how the Native Americans, who once walked through these very woods, came to imagine that supernatural beings were present. An unidentifiable sound, a sudden rush of air, a feeling that one wasn't really alone . . .

Suddenly Miranda stopped, seeing that she really *wasn't* alone. There, up ahead, was the boy from the library. He was sitting on a log in a clearing, seemingly lost in a day-dream as he basked in one of the few bright spots of sunlight that penetrated the dense growth of the forest.

She stood very still, taking a moment to study him. The oblique beams of light glinted off his tousle of golden hair, giving the impression of tiny sparks. His jeans and T-shirt hugged the clearly defined muscles of his body: the broad shoulders, the firm arms, the strong back. His eyes were closed, his face turned upward as he warmed it in the sun. An enraptured expression had settled over his features.

She hesitated to bother him. Yet that same pull she'd felt the other time she'd seen him made it impossible for her to resist. She hesitated for a moment, trying to calm her pounding heart.

"Hello!" she called as she walked toward him.

As he opened his eyes, his look was matter-of-fact, as if somehow he had known she was coming.

She sat down next to him on the log. "I need a rest." She was trying to sound casual. "It's turned out to be pretty warm today."

Miranda leaned her head back and shook out her hair, then twisted it loosely into a coil and pinned it up in a topknot. She could feel him watching her, taking in the smallest gesture. His gaze was admiring. Knowing that, being aware of the power she had over him, gave her an odd, tingling feeling.

He was silent as he continued to study her. Sitting this close to him, their arms and their thighs nearly touching, set Miranda's heart racing again. His face was only inches away from hers. She drew her breath in sharply as she encountered his piercing eyes. She looked away, finding it impossible to meet his penetrating stare.

"You know," she said, "I don't even know your name."

"It's Garth. Garth Gautier."

"And I'm Miranda Campbell."

"I know."

"How did you know that?"

He paused for only a second before answering. "You told me. Last week, the day we met in the library. When I helped you with that book."

She thought back, trying to remember.

"I envy you, you know," she told him.

"Me? Why?"

"Being able to take time off. I'd love the chance to do something like that. All that wonderful freedom . . ."

"And what would you do with 'all that wonderful freedom'?"

Miranda closed her eyes and lifted her face toward the warmth of the sun. "I'd do everything I've ever dreamed of doing. I'd travel all over the world. I'd go live in a big city and study acting. I'd go to the theater every night. I'd read all the books I've always wanted to read but never had the time for. . . ."

She stopped, sighing wistfully. "The only problem is, I'd be afraid of getting lonely."

Garth shrugged. "That doesn't bother me. I've always been kind of a loner."

"I like being by myself sometimes, too." Miranda plucked a twig from the ground and mindlessly began peeling off the bark. "Don't you miss your family and your friends, though?"

"What?" The single syllable came out abruptly.

"Your parents. Your friends from school. They're still up in Portland, aren't they?"

"We stay in touch."

"Do you live nearby?"

"I'm way out on the edge of town. The house is kind of isolated. You may not have even noticed it."

Another long silence followed. Miranda bent over and with the stick began scratching a design of haphazard lines into the moist soil.

"Do you walk in the woods a lot?" she finally asked.

"I feel at home in the woods," he said simply.

"That seems kind of odd. Since you grew up in a city and all."

"I never felt I belonged in the city. I feel as if I belong here, among the trees. Among the birds and the other animals . . ." He stopped himself midsentence. "The woods along the coast have turned out to be one of the best things about moving down here from Portland."

Miranda let out a long, loud sigh. "Overlook's okay, I suppose, but the way I'm feeling, I'd give anything for the chance to jump on the next bus out of here, move someplace like Portland, and get lost in the crowd."

Garth frowned. "Sounds like you want to run away."

She focused on her twig drawing, this time dragging bits of moss across the dirt with her stick to incorporate into her free-form design. "Not really. It's just that these days it seems like everything's falling apart. Everything." She remained absorbed in her doodling for a long time before adding, "My parents just split up."

In a low voice he said, "That must be really tough on you."

She bit her lip. Instead of making her feel better, his kind words made it difficult to fight back self-pitying tears. "That's only part of it. Then there's my boyfriend. Or maybe I should start getting used to thinking of him as my ex-boyfriend."

"You broke up with him?"

Shaking her head, Miranda said, "No one's even dared suggest that. But I can feel him drifting away. There's this other girl,

Amy, but that's only part of it. There's been tension between us lately. . . .

"Oh, sure, we're still going through the motions. We talk on the phone every chance we get, I see him in school. . . . But I can get this sense that something is happening. I can just feel it. And there's nothing I can do to stop it. It's out of my control." In a quiet voice, she added, "I feel so powerless."

Suddenly self-conscious, Miranda leaned forward so that her hair fell into her face, hiding it from his view. "I—I don't know why I'm telling you all this. I don't even know you."

She was silent for a moment before turning to him, this time meeting his intense gaze head-on. In his eyes she saw warmth. Understanding. Acceptance. "But it's funny. I *feel* as if I know you."

It was true. She was drawn to this boy in a way she couldn't explain . . . in a way she'd never experienced before. Being with him instilled in her a sense of serenity. She could sense his acceptance and his understanding. Being with him was like basking in the warm rays of the sun.

At the same time, there was an excitement— a longing—unlike anything she'd ever felt before. Every emotion was magnified, her sense of herself catapulted to an almost surreal level. Never before had she felt so alive. Never before had life seemed so full of possibilities.

As they sat together on the log, their faces were close, so close she could feel his breath on her cheek. All around was the silence of the forest, broken only by the twittering of the birds, their shrill voices seeming to ask a question. Miranda had an almost irresistible urge to lean over and kiss him. The expression on his face was so open, so trusting. . . .

But instead she pulled back. Her cheeks were growing warm. This feeling was so new. She'd never felt so drawn to someone, not with Bobby, not with anyone. Something was happening, something as uncontrollable as the rest of the events of the past few days—so uncontrollable, in fact, that just below the surface of her exhilaration was fear.

He was spending the first dark hours of night as he so often did, roaming around the endless maze of silent, empty rooms. Hearing his own footsteps echo through the cavernous hallways, seeing his own reflection in the grand ballroom lined on one entire wall with mirrors, hearing only his own voice, knowing there was no one to answer. This was what it meant to be lonely.

The house was palatial, a huge estate built almost a hundred years earlier, when his great-grandfather, Claude Gautier, made his fortune in the lumber industry. There were more than thirty rooms in this three-story mansion. Garth knew that well. For months now he had been examining them, spending these long, empty nights exploring each one. There were sitting rooms and drawing rooms, bedrooms, and parlors. All were decorated ornately, in the style of the French kings. Gold-leaf trim around the windows, handpainted murals on the ceilings, thick Oriental carpets and lush velvet curtains.

Yet this glorious mansion had fallen into ruin. The paint was peeling, the wooden floors dull, the rich fabrics tattered and covered with dust. Roaming through the house, he deplored its decay, fantasizing about the happiness and laughter for which it had served as a backdrop during some earlier time. For his great-grandfather the house had signified the realization of a dream, but his children and their children had had no interest in maintaining it. They'd moved to the city, finding the upkeep of a country estate a burden.

What irony, Garth thought bitterly, glancing around at the worn splendor that surrounded him and experiencing a mixture of appreciation and contempt. To think that my great-grandfather built a castle, an entire empire, with the money he made from the woods in this area. That even now I'm able to live off my inheritance from his fortune. Yet as his great-grandson, I'm destined to spend my life burdened with a curse that enslaves me to these forests.

Little remained in the way of furnishings. That was all long gone. Garth himself needed little; still, he mourned the loss of those objects of beauty even as he disdained the family that had acquired them. *His* family. Having been born a Gautier was, after all, what had burdened him with this loathsome curse. While he didn't understand how it had begun, he did understand it had sentenced him to a lifetime of loneliness. Of misery. Of living in the shadows.

Tonight the anger gnawed away at him even more strongly that usual. Again he found himself thinking about her. What a mixture of emotions he'd experienced that afternoon when she'd approached him in the woods. He'd known she was coming, of course. And it wasn't just that he had been able to hear her and pick up her distinctive scent—a mixture of the fragrant soap she used and the subtle fragrance of flowers, as if their petals had been rubbed into her skin. . . .

It was more. Lately a new feeling had been coming upon him, the feeling that the two of them were playing out a script that had been written long before either of them had even walked the earth, a script that led them to each other, dictated that they find each other. . . .

"No!" He spoke aloud, his voice echoing in the eerily silent room.

This was dangerous thinking. To entertain the idea that they could ever be together, to want it so badly that he might allow himself to believe, even for a moment, that it could really happen.

Yet he could not deny his feelings. For the first time in his life, he had fallen in love.

How long he had anticipated this moment. Dreading it, welcoming it; praying it would come, praying it would stay away. He had waited for this, waited for the one person who would test him. He'd suspected that the fragile rhythm he had created, the routine he had fashioned for himself out of chaos, would one day be disrupted. And he'd known, deep in his heart, that when it finally happened, he would have no control over any of it.

How he deplored his wretched condition! To love . . . yet to know he could never act on that love. What misery could be more devastating? What trial more difficult to endure? As he paced up and down the ballroom, his eyes fixed on the green marble floor, he felt as if someone were trying to wrench his heart out of his chest.

Miranda Campbell. To him her name sounded like angels singing. Already it was embedded inside him, even though he might spend the rest of his life trying to banish it. *Miranda.* What was it about her? The openness and honesty with which she spoke to him. The look in her deep-brown eyes, so innocent, yet at the same time so wise. The ability to feel, to know, to understand . . . he sensed that it was all as much a part of her as it was of him.

Maybe, just maybe . . .

No! There it was again. Even before he would allow himself to think such thoughts, he had to put a stop to them. It was impossible. It was too dangerous to imagine that he could ever pretend he was like everyone else. Even to fantasize that there might be someone who could understand, someone who could accept him, was foolish.

Yet already he had stepped over the line. Twice he had reached out to her. He had taken the kind of risk he had sworn all his life he would never take. Writing those poems, even without putting his name to them, was enough to put himself in peril of overstepping the boundaries designed to keep his secret safe. Still, he hadn't been able to resist. Seeing her, feeling her pain, had made him forget all his resolve. For the moment, nothing had mattered but her . . . and his feelings for her. The love he was now carrying in his heart had blinded him, obscured all the rational thoughts that had made it possible for him to survive so far.

Suddenly an idea came to him. He ran out of the ballroom, heading down the long corridors toward his bedroom. There, he flung open the closet door and dragged out the wooden crate. It was massive, easily four feet high, and so wide that it was a struggle to ease it through the doorway. He had found it when he first came to this house, one of the few things that hadn't been stolen, sold, or destroyed. He'd pried it open with ease, the well-worn wood offering little resistance to his strength.

Inside were countless treasures. Old things, mostly, wonderful trinkets that once upon a time had belonged to someone in his family, a woman. He didn't know her name; it didn't matter. What did matter was that he finally knew what he would do with them. They were worthy of a princess. And he had found that princess.

He took out each item, one at a time, handling them all gently, lovingly. A hard-carved wooden jewelry case, the palest pink trimmed with gold leaf. A delicate figurine, a young shepherd tending two timid lambs. Not every object was beautiful. Wrapped in tissue paper was a Native American mask, a grotesquely distorted face so bizarre that it elicited a deep, primal fear.

There were other things as well, beautiful things, mostly, fine things. Too good for just anyone. But perfect for her. His heart pounding, he studied them all, spread out before him on the thick rug. He considered every piece, trying to see each one through her eyes. After a long deliberation, he finally made his choice.

Yes, he was taking a risk. He knew that. But he still believed he could keep it under control. He could express his love for her. He could be a part of her life. He would simply have to be careful never to let her find out. She must never even suspect. He had been a master of deceit for so long—for almost four years now, ever since he had learned the truth about himself. Surely he could continue even as he dared to reach out.

He felt fired by his resolve. Yes, he was determined to continue. And he would be so careful that no one, not even she, would ever guess the truth.

CHAPTER
6

"I still haven't decided what to wear." Corinne sighed as she set down her lunch tray. "Paul's favorite color is blue, so I guess I should go with that."

Selina wrinkled her nose. "I'll probably end up wearing that same green minidress I wore to my parents' anniversary party. I'd love to get something new, but my mom said no way. Tommy'll just have to put up with a recycled outfit."

Miranda heard snippets of Corinne and Selina's conversation as she made her way across the school cafeteria toward them. The girls' discussion about *Saint Joan* a few days earlier had left behind a tension that continued to hang over her like a cloud.

"Hi," she said in a guarded tone, approaching their table. The orange plastic tray on which she balanced her lunch acted as a kind of shield against the subtle hostility Miranda still felt coming from her two best friends. "Got room for one more?"

Selina and Corinne exchanged looks. There was an uncomfortable pause before Selina said, "Sure."

Miranda sat down and immediately began busying herself with opening her carton of milk and drizzling dressing over her salad. She made a point of keeping her eyes down. Both other girls were silent, watching her.

"We were just talking about the Homecoming Dance," Selina finally said.

Miranda glanced up, surprised. She'd forgotten all about Homecoming. Now, hearing her friends talk about it, she realized it was only three days away. "Oh, right."

"Going, Miranda?" Corinne asked. Her eyes were fixed on her plate.

"I'm not sure," Miranda said, suddenly uncomfortable. "Bobby and I haven't talked about it yet."

Once again, Selina and Corinne exchanged meaningful glances.

"So what are you going to wear?" Miranda asked casually.

Selina piped up, "I was just telling Corinne I'll probably end up wearing the same dress I wore to my parents' anniversary party." Suddenly her green eyes grew large and her hands flew to her face. "Oh, Miranda! I'm so *sorry*!"

Miranda could feel the color drain out of her face. "So I guess you've heard."

Nodding, Selina said, "Bobby said something about it. He just figured Corinne and I would already know."

Miranda swallowed hard. "I'd planned to tell you. It's just that, well, it's still kind of hard for me to talk about it."

"So, Miranda," Corinne said abruptly, changing the subject. "All ready for the audition?"

"Not yet." Miranda tried to keep her tone light. "But I'm working on it."

"Corinne is too," Selina reported. "I've been helping her learn her lines—"

Miranda glanced at her, and was surprised by how betrayed she felt. Still, she made no comment.

"Anyway, it'll be interesting to see who gets the part," Selina went on, glossing over the accidental confession.

"Of course," said Corinne, "it's still not too

late for you to reconsider whether or not you want to go through all the bother of auditioning."

So it's really true, Miranda thought, *our friendship has come to this.* "I'm with Selina," Miranda said with resolve. "I'll be interested in seeing who ends up with the part."

She suspected that between now and the audition the following evening, she'd be able to think about little else.

As she made her way toward Bobby's locker, Miranda was furious at Corinne and Selina, but she'd made up her mind about the Homecoming Dance. Not only would she go, she would have the time of her life. She deserved to let loose, to have some fun. An evening of dancing, laughing, and seeing her *other* friends was exactly what she needed.

Bobby was alone, she was happy to see, without his usual entourage of basketball buddies surrounding him.

"Hi, Bobby!" she said, determined to forget about Corinne and Selina.

He turned, but instead of looking pleased to see her, she saw there was something else written on his face. Something she couldn't quite read. "Hey, Miranda."

She decided she was just being paranoid and forged ahead. "I guess you've heard about the dance Friday night."

He swallowed hard. "Uh, look, Miranda. There's something you and I need to talk about."

There was a coldness in his tone that frightened her. And made her feel as if he were suddenly far, far away.

"Okay," Miranda said, trying to keep her voice even.

Bobby glanced around the crowded corridor in frustration. "This isn't exactly the best place—"

"What is it, Bobby? Tell me."

He looked her square in the face. "Look, Miranda. Maybe all we need is a little time apart. You know, to think about things, figure some stuff out . . ."

All of a sudden Miranda became aware of the presence of someone else, directly behind her.

"Hello, Bobby."

Annoyed, Miranda glanced over her shoulder. "Hello, Amy." It took everything she had to keep her voice controlled.

The blond girl swept her hair over one

shoulder and stretched her mouth into a fake, sickly-sweet smile.

"Miranda, don't you have a class to get to?"

Bobby answered for her. "Sixth period doesn't start for another five minutes, Amy. Besides, Miranda and I are trying to talk."

"Well, this will just take a minute."

"What is it?" Bobby said, obviously very uncomfortable.

"I just wanted to know what time you're picking me up for the Homecoming Dance."

Miranda looked over at Bobby, expecting him to laugh at what was really a very bad joke.

"Bobby?" she said.

He looked down at the floor. Suddenly Miranda turned, pushing through the crowd of laughing students, wishing she could keep on running without ever having to stop.

I've got to get away, Miranda thought as she raced blindly toward her bicycle. All she wanted to do was ride into the wind, to push her legs hard against the pedals, as if by doing so she could somehow manage to push away the onslaught of sadness and confusion.

She'd known something was wrong, that the special ties she and Bobby had once had to each other were unraveling. The rational, clear-thinking part of her had seen it coming. Still, confronting it head-on was more painful than she ever could have imagined. She kept picturing the smug look on Amy Patterson's face. . . . And the guilty one on Bobby's.

She slowed down as she turned the corner of the school building. Her bicycle, chained to the rack where she'd left it, was a welcome sight. But something was different.

She quickened her pace. There was a crinkled brown paper bag in the basket, so unremarkable that most people would have found it barely worth a second glance. Yet she knew.

Holding her breath, she reached inside and pulled out a round gold box. The top, curved like a dome, was studded with jewels, red, blue, and green stones that glinted in the sunlight. It was easily more beautiful than anything she'd ever held in her hand.

Gently she pulled off the lid. She wasn't at all surprised to find a piece of paper inside, folded into quarters. Holding the gold box next to her heart, she read.

> *Like glowing stars and golden sun,*
> *Like sands of desert and the sea,*
> *Like dust of snow and summer rain,*
> *Together we can never be.*

CHAPTER
7

"'Together we can never be,'" Miranda repeated as she rode her bike across the bumpy schoolyard. She was beginning to understand that her mystery man was hiding more than just his identity. He was harboring a secret, something that had doomed their relationship before it had even begun.

But as exhilarating as it was to know someone was out there who truly admired her and cared about her, it was also enormously frustrating. If they could never be together, what was the point of his lavishing this attention on her? She was caught up in what seemed an impossible situation.

All of a sudden she speeded up, knowing exactly what she was going to do. She'd seek out someone real, someone who was more than a mere fantasy. She headed for the library.

Adrenaline flowed through her as she strode inside. He was there, exactly as she'd hoped. This time she found Garth in the stacks. He was returning a book to its place on one of the uppermost shelves. She glanced up, noticing its title: *Folklore of the Pacific Northwest.*

"Hello, again," she said, resisting the urge to just stand there unseen, watching him.

Instead of looking surprised at her unexpected appearance, he simply glanced over. "Hello."

Miranda was suddenly filled with apprehensions about what she planned to do. She was tempted to turn and run, but the pull—far greater than her own fears—was too strong. "Can I talk to you for a minute? There's something I want to ask you."

"Of course." Garth glanced around. There were a few people sitting at nearby tables. "Let's find someplace we can talk."

With a nod, Miranda followed him to a small study tucked away along the back wall of the main room. Her confident walk belied her nervousness. Once the door was closed, she perched on the edge of one of the carrels.

"Is everything all right?" Garth's blue eyes were clouded with concern.

"Everything is fine." Miranda took a deep breath. "Actually, I'm here to extend an invitation."

"An invitation?"

"That's right. There's a Homecoming Dance at my school this Friday night, and, well, I was wondering if you'd like to go with me."

She held her breath as she waited for his reaction, unable to look away from his face.

"A school dance?"

Miranda bit her lip. "You don't want to go, do you? I know; it's too silly. Now that you're out of high school . . ."

"No, no. It's not that. It's just—"

"What?" Miranda urged.

Garth looked uncomfortable. "I—I'm not much of a dancer."

"Is *that* all?" She hesitated. "Well, if you want to know the truth, I'm not either. But I'll make a deal with you. I promise not to complain about you stepping on my feet if you do the same for me."

A smile crept slowly over his face. "You're a hard person to say no to."

"Good. The dance starts at eight."

"I'll pick you up at quarter of."

"I live at—"

"I know where you live."

Miranda blinked in surprise. "You do?"

A flush rose up on Garth's cheeks. He hesitated, then leaned forward slightly as if he were going to say something. Looking into his blue eyes, she saw an intensity that left her breathless.

And then he looked away. The moment had passed.

"Well, then," she said, after swallowing hard, "I guess I'll see you Friday."

"Friday."

As Miranda gazed into Garth's penetrating blue eyes, Friday seemed an eternity away.

She was gone.

As he watched her sail out of the library, he experienced a sort of pain, as if something that were part of him had been wrenched away. What had before seemed an ordinary room now felt confining, ominous somehow, the air so heavy he could hardly breathe.

Miranda. Her name filled his head like some magical incantation. Yet mingled with the euphoria was fear. Part of him stood back, observing, disapproving. Watching him do what he'd sworn never to do.

Letting her in. Slowly, gradually allowing her to become part of his life.

He had never intended to let this happen. Yet saying no to her was unthinkable. He was powerless before her. Overwhelmed. While logic and reason warned him to resist, in her presence he knew only that this intoxicating feeling was something he needed. Something from which he could draw the strength to continue to fight, battling against what he knew to be devastating odds.

Something without which he could not survive.

Now, it was done. He had opened the door, agreed to let her in, if only for one short evening. It was a tremendous risk. Part of him warned himself to put a stop to what he was putting in motion, now, before it was too late.

Another part rejoiced.

Still, something nagged at him. There was something he needed to find out, a question he had to answer. A feeling of dread weighed him down as he headed toward the library's reference area. He was nearly immobilized by the task that loomed before him, his usually limitless energy sapped as he sought out what he had to know.

It didn't take long for him to find the book he needed.

His heart was pounding as he opened the almanac, the compact volume oddly heavy in his hand. He leafed through it until he found the right section. Printed on a calendar were tiny circles, shaded in to indicate the different phases of the moon. New moon, crescent moon, half moon, gibbous moon . . .

He ran his finger down the page, stopping it on Friday, just three days away. He froze.

Panic and terror rose up in him as he frantically checked the month. Yes, he had the right month. Then he looked again at day. Friday, it read, seeming to mock him.

From deep inside, a howl threatened to push its way through his lungs, disrupting the stillness of the library. It took everything he had to keep it inside.

He looked again, still hoping he'd been wrong. Perhaps he had missed something. Perhaps he'd made a mistake. Perhaps . . . perhaps . . .

But there was no mistake. The small white circle, unmarred by even a sliver of black, showed that his calculations were accurate, just as they always were.

His worst fears had been realized. This

Friday—the night of the dance, the night of his date with Miranda—was also the night of the full moon.

Miranda felt giddy as she pedaled away from the library. *I did it!* she was thinking, still barely able to believe her own boldness. Asking Garth to the dance made her feel she was embarking on a new beginning, one filled with infinite possibilities.

And to think that only that morning, she had considered herself Bobby's girlfriend. How far away that seemed now! The scene with Amy, Bobby's suggestion that they spend some time apart, clearly just an easy way for him to tell her it was over, the anger and mortification she'd felt . . . Now all she felt was relief. The attentions—however mysterious—of her secret admirer combined with the powerful pull she felt toward Garth had suddenly made it clear to Miranda that her feelings for Bobby were not as deep as she'd imagined.

Miranda was too keyed up to go home, particularly to what had begun to feel like a sad, lonely house. Instead she steered her bicycle toward an inland section of Overlook, making a few turns until she found herself in front of a small but well-manicured house with the name "Clay" painted on the mailbox.

Elinor's mother answered the door, ushering her inside and then going off to call her daughter. Miranda stood awkwardly in the foyer. She'd known Elinor casually for more than three years—they'd been in a few classes together—but Miranda had never dropped in on her like this before.

Any doubts she may have had about whether or not she'd be welcome were put to rest as Elinor greeted her. "Miranda? What a nice surprise."

"Are you busy?" Miranda took in the outfit Elinor was wearing, a pair of old jeans and a baggy sweater. Her straight, light-brown hair was pulled back in a ponytail, a few loose strands falling into her face. "If I'm interrupting anything, I could—"

"No, no. Not at all. I was just out back raking leaves. I was about ready for a break. Come in and have some hot chocolate."

Elinor led the way into the kitchen. Miranda sat down at the table, glancing around at the bright room, painted a cheerful shade of yellow with blue-and-white striped curtains on the window above the sink. It looks like the kitchen of a happy family, Miranda thought, comparing it to her own kitchen, which had lately seemed so dark and depressing.

Elinor turned on the kettle, then joined her at the kitchen table. "I'll bet you're excited," she said, "with the auditions all set for tomorrow night."

Miranda nodded. "I've been rehearsing my lines every spare moment I could grab."

"You'll do great."

"I hope so. I'd love the chance to be in this play."

"Well, I'll be in the wings, rooting for you."

You're the only one who will be, Miranda thought, reminded suddenly of Corinne and Selina. Then she remembered Garth.

"Are you going to the dance Friday night?"

"I hadn't been planning to." Elinor shrugged. "I'm not big on that sort of thing. How about you?"

"Oh, Elinor," Miranda said, unable to contain her excitement any longer. "I can't believe what I just did."

"What?"

Miranda's tone was wistful as she said, "I've met the most incredible guy in the world, and I just asked him to the dance."

Elinor's hazel eyes widened. "Who is he, Miranda? Somebody at school?"

"No. He's a little bit older. His name is Garth Gautier, and I met him at the library in town. He's doing some kind of research there. He's originally from Portland, but now that he's graduated from high school he's taking some time off to decide what he wants to do."

"I guess I'd better start paying closer attention at the library! What's he like?"

Miranda thought for a few seconds. "Well . . . he's smart . . . sensitive . . . kind. And there's something slightly mysterious about him." She laughed self-consciously. "I'm not doing a very good job of describing him. But I've never felt this way about anybody. I know I barely know him, but I just feel we belong together. There's something about him, Elinor, something I can't quite put my finger on. Something . . . *special.*"

"He must be, if you're so crazy about him."

Miranda's cheeks were hot. "It shows that much?"

Elinor laughed. "You could say that. As a matter of fact, maybe I'll come to that dance just so I can check him out."

"Why don't you? It should be fun. And why don't you ask somebody you like?"

"Hmmm." A broad smile crossed Elinor's face. "Do you know Ricky Garcia?"

"Sure. He's a good friend of Bobby's. They're on the basketball team together."

"I've always thought he was kind of cute. . . . Do you know if he's going out with anybody?"

The kettle began to whistle then. Elinor jumped up, reaching for a pot holder.

"You know what they say," Miranda told her with a smile. "There's only one way to find out."

CHAPTER
8

The auditions for *Saint Joan* were being held at the Overlook Playhouse, an old theater nestled in the hills on the outskirts of town. The theater, a focal point for the people of the town since the 1800s, and now the home of the Pacific Players, rose dramatically from the uneven terrain, and was surrounded by a circle of tall, fragrant pine trees.

As Miranda passed through the empty lobby, she noted the framed posters advertising the theater company's past productions: Ibsen's *A Doll's House*, Chekhov's *The Cherry Orchard*, Beckett's *Waiting for Godot*. Her heels made a sharp rapping sound against the marble floor. Miranda took a moment to catch her breath before pulling open the door into the theater itself. She was nervous; reciting a

monologue in a classroom was one thing, but
having to say those same words on a real
stage, in front of a real director, was something else entirely.

At least she was confident about the way
she looked.

She'd agonized over what to wear, wanting
something that would show up well on the
stage without looking too showy. In the end
she'd settled on black stretch pants and an
oversize shirt made from a silky raspberry-
colored fabric that shimmered when she
moved.

"How do I look, Mom?" she'd asked,
standing proudly before her mother.

"Oh, are you going out tonight?" Miranda's mother had said as she looked up
from her magazine. "Have a nice time,
honey."

The wave of disappointment that had
washed over Miranda seemed far away as she
took one more deep breath and pushed
open the heavy wooden door that opened
into the theater. She'd been expecting a
mob scene. Instead, only twenty or thirty
people were milling around, their faces
bright and eager as they chatted with one another.

Miranda was not surprised to see that most of them were adults. Some she recognized from the three or four Pacific Players productions she'd seen. She scanned the faces in the crowd. She was particularly interested in the women, anxious to see who else might be trying out for the lead role, the only female part in the play. Her anxiety increased as she spotted two seniors, Maura Malone and Jill Wright, who had taken theater the year before. Miranda slipped into the nearest seat, aware that her self-confidence was seeping away.

"And now, the star of our show . . ."

She whirled around in response to the voice she'd heard behind her. "Elinor! Hi!"

"Ready to knock 'em dead?"

"I hope so." Miranda grimaced. "I keep telling myself it's only a play. But I'm still a nervous wreck!"

"You'll be fine. Once you get up there, you'll forget to be nervous. Besides, I'll be watching from the wings, keeping my fingers crossed."

"Thanks, Elinor." Miranda's tone was sincere.

"Better run. Break a leg!"

When Corinne walked in a few minutes

later, Miranda started. She watched as the tall
blond girl glanced around the theater, spotted Miranda—and then made a point of sitting way over on the other side.

As she was debating whether or not to go
over and talk to her, Tyler Fleming, the director, clapped his hands. He was a tall,
lanky man with long dark hair pulled back
into a ponytail, a slender nose, and high,
chiseled cheekbones that gave him a gaunt
look. His already dramatic looks were emphasized by the black turtleneck he wore
with his jeans.

"All right, everybody, please take a seat in
the first six rows. I'd like to get started."

Miranda glanced over at Corinne as she
made her way toward the front. Corinne had
already moved to another row, once again sitting at the opposite end of the theater.
Miranda found a seat on the center aisle,
missing the old Corinne who would have sat
with her at an audition like this, cheering her
on even as they competed for the same part.

She was relieved when Tyler Fleming
again clapped his hands. "Welcome, and
thank you all for coming tonight. We're already running a few minutes behind, so I'd
like to move things right along. The part

we'll be auditioning first is the lead, Joan of Arc, after whom the play is named. The character is one of the strongest in the history of theater. Joan is brave, determined, and unwavering in her conviction that she must carry out the special mission for which she has been chosen. As a symbol, she represents one lonely voice taking on a struggle that would defeat anyone who lacked her magnificent courage.

"Above all, the Maid of Orléans stands alone. She and only she can carry out the task set forth for her by the highest powers. She has been chosen, and she must overcome all obstacles to fulfill her destiny."

Tyler Fleming glanced around the auditorium. With a chuckle, he added, "Quite a lot for a seventeen-year-old girl to take on."

As he spoke, Miranda's nervousness was evolving into excitement. She could hardly wait to get up on that stage. To play a young woman with such a strong belief in herself . . . Miranda longed to be someone as pure of heart and as full of conviction as Joan of Arc—even if it was only for two short hours at a time.

"All right." Tyler Fleming glanced at the clipboard his assistant had just handed him.

"Let's begin with Maura Malone. Maura, where are you?"

Maura gave a good reading, although she kept twirling a strand of her reddish-brown hair around her finger as she pleaded with Charles VII to allow her to free France and see him crowned king. Jill Wright was next. She, too, was clear and forceful, although she stumbled over her words as she read the scene in which Saint Joan performs a miracle: changing the wind's direction.

Finally Tyler Fleming called Miranda's name. She rose up out of her seat, feeling the eyes of everyone in the auditorium upon her. Yet, as she walked toward the stage, any lingering traces of nervousness vanished. She was no longer Miranda Campbell. She was a French girl called Joan, preparing to meet her fate head-on.

The scene she'd chosen to read was from the beginning of the play, in which Joan announces that voices have instructed her to acquire an army to battle the English at Orléans. The dramatic scene established Joan's strength and determination. As Miranda recited the lines she'd memorized, she found her awareness of the audience and even the director slipping away. She moved comfortably about the stage, responding naturally to the lines Tyler Fleming fed her. It was almost as if the real Saint Joan were speaking through her.

When she reached the end of the scene, she felt disoriented, and needed a few seconds to remember where and who she was. The burst of applause jolted her back to the present.

"Brava!" someone called from the first few rows of the auditorium.

Joan of Arc had disappeared and in her place was a self-conscious Miranda. "Thank you," she muttered, hurrying off the stage.

"Very nice." Tyler Fleming pronounced the words slowly, as if he'd been surprised by the passion with which Miranda had delivered her lines. Miranda simply nodded, then slid down in her seat.

"We have one more person trying out for the role of Saint Joan," the director went on. Checking his clipboard, he called, "Corinne Davis."

As Corinne made her way down the aisle, Miranda was more nervous than she'd been before her own reading.

Corinne took her place in the center of the stage, her head held high and her shoulders squared. Instead of jumping right in, however, she took a moment to skim the pages of script. Miranda noticed she was clutching the book in her hand, and when she looked in her eyes, she knew that Corinne was terrified. Miranda's heart went out to her. "It's okay, Corinne," she said softly. "Just take a deep breath and you'll be fine."

"Whenever you're ready," the director finally said, a trifle impatient. "Which scene are you reading?"

Corinne looked out over the hushed audience. "The scene where Joan finds out she's going to be burned at the stake." Her voice sounded strained.

The director waited a few seconds, then said, "Would you like me to start you off? I could read the inquisitor's line on page one hundred twelve—"

"No, that's okay." Standing stiffly, Corinne began haltingly, her voice so soft that even those in the front row leaned forward in an attempt to hear.

Miranda's stomach tightened as the thick tension grew in the auditorium. No one moved a muscle or dared to whisper. It was as if every aspiring actor in the room were experiencing Corinne's stage fright, suffering through every endless moment right along with her. "Come on, Corinne . . ."

Almost as if she were responding to Miranda's plea, Corinne's nervousness began to slip away. As she gained confidence, her voice became clear and resonant, her gestures more natural. With passion and fluidity she spoke the words of the courageous heroine, bringing to life the scene in which Joan clings to her convictions even though doing so means accepting the hideous fate of being burned at the stake.

When she'd finished, Miranda joined the others in their enthusiastic applause. She tried to catch Corinne's eye as she came off the stage, wanting to share a triumphant smile. But Corinne never even looked in her direction.

"Very nice, Corinne. Thank you very much." Tyler Fleming turned to the rest of the troupe. "That wraps it up for the part of Saint Joan. Thank you, ladies. I'll be announcing the cast list in a few days. Next we'll hear readings for the part of Charles VII. . . ."

Miranda followed Corinne as she headed out of the theater. "Corinne, wait up!"

Corinne glanced over her shoulder. Reluctantly she stopped. "What is it?"

"I just wanted to tell you what a terrific job you did."

"Surprised?"

"No, of course not. I just—"

"Look, Miranda," Corinne said, tossing her mane of gold-streaked hair. "You and I both gave good readings. Certainly better than Maura and Jill. Now all we have to do is wait for Mr. Fleming to make his decision."

Miranda nodded. "I just hope that, no matter how it comes out, this play doesn't get in the way of our friendship." She searched Corinne's face hopefully. "Don't you agree that no matter who wins and who loses, we can survive this?"

"It depends," Corinne replied.

"On what?"

Corinne pushed open the door, letting in a rush of icy night air. "Which one of us wins . . . and which one of us loses."

The next morning, making her way through the corridors at school, her books clutched against her chest, Miranda was finding it difficult to focus on the classes ahead of her. Thank goodness it was a half-day—there was some teachers conference or something. She was only vaguely aware of the crush of students all around her, filling the hallways as they hurried to their lockers or to homeroom. Instead, she was wrapped up in thinking about the audition.

How magical it had been, being onstage! Pretending she was Joan of Arc, one of the most romantic historical figures of all time. Reciting the poetic words of George Bernard Shaw, hearing them come to life. Feeling every pair of eyes in the room focused upon her. Being given the chance to shine, to do something she had always longed to do . . . it had all been so wonderful. And the magnficent feeling had stayed with her all night, casting her in a glow that even her mother had noticed.

"How did the audition go?" Mrs. Campbell had asked eagerly the moment Miranda let herself into the house. She'd been sitting in the living room, as if she'd been waiting for her to come home.

"Oh, Mom! It was great!" Miranda fell onto the living-room couch, leaning her head back against a throw pillow. "Just great!"

"Were you nervous?"

"Well, maybe a little. But it hardly mattered at all. Once I was up there onstage, standing in front of the audience, concentrating on being someone else, I forgot all about being nervous. I forgot everything. Mom, I know it sounds crazy, but I actually *became* Joan of Arc!"

"It doesn't sound crazy at all." Her mother laughed. "In fact, it sounds absolutely fabulous. I'm glad you had fun, honey."

Miranda sighed. "I loved every minute."

"And . . ." Mrs. Campbell hesitated before asking, "Did you get the part?"

"I don't know yet. It's going to take Tyler Fleming, the director, a few days to decide. But I've got a really good feeling about this."

"I wish you the best of luck."

" 'Break a leg' is what they say in the theater."

"Yes, of course." There was another long pause before Mrs. Campbell spoke again. "By the way, Miranda, I owe you an apology."

"An apology?" She sat upright, looking over at her mother. "What for?"

"For forgetting what a special night this was for you." Mrs. Campbell brushed a strand of hair out of her eyes. "I know I should have remembered this was the date of the audition. And I'm sorry. It's just that I've been so distracted lately, given everything that's been going on between your father and me. . . ."

"I understand," Miranda said softly. "And it's okay, Mom. Really it is."

Seeing the troubled look on her mother's face, noting the lines creasing her forehead, Miranda's heart constricted. She really did understand. Her mother had her own conflicts to deal with.

At that moment, she felt closer to her mother than she ever had before. Instead of simply being mother and daughter, she had a sense that they were two kindred spirits, both of them leading parallel lives in which the best they could do for each other was simply be there.

That night as she slept, Miranda's dreams had been filled with images from the different aspects of her life, all merging and coming apart in peculiar ways. She was about to go onstage, but hadn't yet learned her lines. Both her parents were in the audience, sitting separately. Her friends were there too: Selina, Corinne, even Elinor. And Bobby was there, sitting with his arm around Amy, who was wearing a smug expression. In the dream, she realized that knowing so many of the people in the theater should have made performing easier. Instead, it was making it more difficult.

Now, as she stood in front of her locker

distractedly turning the combination, all the confusion and anxiety that had plagued Miranda the night before had faded. Instead, she was basking in the joy she'd felt about being part of a real theatrical troupe.

If only I get the part! she was thinking. If only, if only . . .

Suddenly, before Miranda knew what was happening, she felt something push against her shoulder. Her schoolbooks went flying and her shoulder bag slid to the floor. Within seconds the loose sheets of papers that had been tucked into one of her spiral notebooks were strewn everywhere.

"What on *earth* . . . ?"

She whirled around and found herself looking into the smirking face of Andy Swensen.

"Oops. Sorry about that, Miranda. Guess I'm getting clumsy in my old age."

Standing behind him were Dave Falco, his arms folded across his chest, and Mark O'Neill, leaning against the line of metal lockers. They, too, were grinning.

"What's your problem?"

"Hey, it wasn't my fault!" Andy insisted. "Mark pushed me."

"Yeah, right," Mark said.

Dave began to laugh.

"Look," Miranda said impatiently. "If you want to horse around, go find someplace else to—"

"You heard the lady," Andy jeered. "No horsing around!" He reached over and punched Mark in the shoulder.

The other boy's grin faded. "Hey, cool it, will you?"

"Oh, yeah?" Andy hit his friend again, this time in the chest.

Miranda glanced around, wishing someone would come along and help her put a stop to this. But even though the halls were filled with students, no one seemed to notice.

With a sigh, she crouched down and began picking up her books and papers.

"Hey, Miranda, that was some stunt you pulled with Wexler the other day. He's still on my case."

Glancing up at Andy, she mumbled, "I didn't mean to get you in trouble."

"'I didn't mean to get you in trouble,'" Andy mimicked her in a high-pitched voice. His two friends burst into loud guffaws. Miranda could feel her cheeks growing red.

"Hey, what's this?" Andy bent down and grabbed a sheaf of the paper that had fallen to the ground. " 'Notes on *Romeo and Juliet*,' " he read.

"Give me those," Miranda said, standing up.

"Hey, check this out, guys." Andy pulled the pile of papers away so it was just out of her reach.

"Andy, I need those notes." She was trying hard to keep her voice calm.

"They must be really important if she wants them back so badly," Mark jeered.

"Yes, they're important," said Miranda. "I spent an entire afternoon at the library, taking those notes. Now, if you don't mind, I—"

"Wexler's English project, huh? What could be more boring than William Shakespeare?" Suddenly a peculiar glint lit up Andy's dark eyes. "Hey, wait a second. On second thought, these could turn out to be useful."

Miranda's stomach was churning. "Andy, please. This isn't funny anymore."

"Maybe I could save myself some time," Andy went on. "*Romeo and Juliet*, huh? Sure, I could write a paper on that. Maybe I'll even ace the course."

"Yeah, right," Mark scoffed. "That'll be the day."

Suddenly Miranda turned to face him.

"Why are you doing this, Andy? Why are you picking on me?"

"Maybe he's got a crush on you," Dave teased. "Maybe Andy here's dying to ask you to the dance tomorrow night."

"Yeah, right!" Andy's tone was scornful.

"Yeah, maybe he is," Mark seconded. "But maybe he's afraid you'd turn him down."

"Probably would, too," said Dave. "Miranda probably thinks she's too good to go out with Andy."

"Hey, guys. Give me a break. I could do a lot better than going to that stupid dance with a girl as stuck-up as Miranda Campbell." Andy was trying to keep his tone light, but Miranda could see there was a hard look in his dark eyes as he glanced at her appraisingly.

"For your information, I already have a date." Miranda took a step toward him, reaching for the notes. "Now, if you don't mind—"

"Maybe I'll hang on to these a while." Andy was already folding up the pages and sticking them into his back pocket. "You're an A student, Miranda. Maybe I can improve my mind by seeing how somebody like you does such a good job of kissing up to all the teachers."

"Andy, give those back!"

Miranda's plea went unacknowledged. The three boys had already turned and were walking away, laughing loudly and punching each other in a playful way. As Andy disappeared around the corner with his pals, she could see the papers sticking out of his back pocket, an odd, misshapen wad.

Miranda dropped her pencil onto her desk, letting out a loud sigh. As annoyed as she was at Andy Swenson for stealing her notes, she was still determined to make a good start on her English project. She'd already spent an hour after school trying to reconstruct her notes and was ready for a break.

Since morning it had been foggy and gray. Now it was almost two o'clock. When she went over to the window and saw that the clouds had dissolved to reveal a clear blue sky, she threw open the window. What had begun as a gloomy day had turned sunny and warm with a refreshing undercurrent of crisp autumn air.

Tucking away her notes, she changed out of the skirt she'd worn to school, putting on a pair of jeans, sneakers, and a thick fisherman's sweater. She ran downstairs and was about to head out the door when the telephone rang.

"Garth!" she cried once she recognized his voice. "What a nice surprise!"

"Surprises are the order of the day," he replied. "I happen to have one of my own in mind. That is, if you don't already have plans for this afternoon."

"I'm free as a bird," she told him. "In fact, I was just heading out to the woods for a walk. It's such a perfect day—"

"Good. Then perhaps I can convince you to meet me—in, shall we say, ten minutes?"

"I'd love to. But what's the surprise?"

"Ah. You'll simply have to wait to find out. Otherwise it won't be a surprise."

He suggested that they meet by a huge cedar tree, one she knew well, on the edge of Overlook. Before dashing out the door, Miranda gave her hair a good brushing.

As she walked toward the place where she and Garth had agreed to meet, Miranda looked around, taking in the perfect fall day. The tall, dignified evergreens that edged Overlook stood proudly against the cloudless sky, the same blue as robins' eggs. Interspersed among the cedars, dotting the horizon, were thick clumps of deciduous trees,

their leaves a brilliant collage of bright oranges, vibrant yellows, and flaming reds, colors as intense as fire.

After checking her watch for the fifth time
since she'd left the house, she quickened her
pace. Now that she was on the verge of meeting him, she was suddenly impatient.

Her curiosity about Garth's surprise was
only part of it. Even more, she was looking
forward to spending time with the quiet, mysterious boy from the library. Despite her con-
stant resolve to keep her romantic notions in
check, her continual warnings to herself that
she didn't even know him, she couldn't help
being intrigued.

Usually Miranda prided herself on having
a well-developed sense of people. She had a
knack for evaluating strangers, even those
about whom she had very little information.
She'd mastered the art of forming opinions
that in the long run turned out to be accurate. It was second nature to her, figuring out
what someone she'd just met was all about—
and Garth Gautier was no exception.

Her initial impression of him had been
that behind the brooding exterior was a
deep, sensitive young man. He also struck
her as exceptionally intelligent. Whether or

not he was the type of person who did well in school, she couldn't say. But she suspected he was quick-witted in terms of his perceptions. That, she could see in his eyes. It was right there, in that way he had of looking at her, a way that made her feel he already knew everything there was to know about her.

She couldn't deny that there was something else as well. Something physical. From the very first time she'd seen Garth Gautier, she'd felt drawn to him in a way she'd never experienced before. Not even with Bobby had she had such a strong reaction. Simply standing close to him as they stood in the narrow passageway between the bookshelves at the library had caused her adrenaline to race, her heart to pound, her blood to rush through her body. Miranda longed to touch him, to feel the warmth of his skin, the soft texture of his hair, the hardness of his shoulders. . . .

"Silly girl!" she teased herself, speaking aloud. "You sound like a kid with a crush."

Still, as she walked she could feel her cheeks burning. And she was fully aware that the steep hills of Overlook were only partly responsible for the warmth that suddenly rushed over her as she realized she was now only a few hundred yards away from their meeting place.

Sure enough; she turned a corner and saw him standing there, patiently waiting for her. He was dressed in jeans and his gray suede jacket, his hair the same thick tousle of unruly curls. In one hand he held a wicker picnic basket. He was also carrying a blanket, soft flannel printed with a bright red plaid, and a portable tape player.

"Let me guess . . ." Miranda said, smiling as she greeted him.

His serious expression melted, and he looked suddenly hopeful. "A late lunch. I hope it's all right."

"I love picnics. But I wish you'd told me what you had in mind. I could've helped." Glancing at the basket he was holding, she added, "But it looks as if you've thought of everything."

He nodded. "I hope so." Then, as if deciding suddenly to put his shyness aside for the afternoon, he said, "I consider this a very important occasion. And having a picnic is only part of it. I'm really looking forward to the opportunity to get to know you."

He hesistated before adding, "You know, I was very flattered that you asked me to the dance. I've never had a girl ask me out on a date before."

"I've never asked a boy out before, either."

"You seemed so at ease . . . was it difficult?"

"Less than I'd expected."

Miranda averted her eyes. All of a sudden she felt shy. This new boy, someone she barely knew, had clearly put a great deal of thought into making this afternoon memorable for both of them. Was it possible that he felt the same excitement she did about the prospect of spending time together?

In an attempt at overcoming her sudden awkwardness, she gestured toward the things he was holding. "You look as if you brought along everything except the kitchen sink! What exactly do you have there?"

"Hopefully, everything we'll need for a perfect afternoon." He glanced up at the cloudless sky. "That is, as long as this great weather holds up. And since it looks as if Mother Nature intends to be cooperative, we should do fine." His blue eyes shining mischievously, Garth added, "You know, there's a real art to planning a picnic."

"An art you appeared to have mastered," Miranda said, only half teasing.

"It's taken years of study. But the way I see

it, having the perfect picnic is simply a question of fulfilling the four most basic human needs."

He was standing very close to Miranda, his eyes fixed intently on hers. Out in the bright sunlight, she saw they were even bluer than they'd appeared under the fluorescent lights inside the library. She could feel herself growing flushed. When a sudden gust of wind blew her hair into her eyes, she was relieved to have an excuse to look away.

"The four most basic human needs," she repeated, her voice hoarse. "And what are they?"

"I'll tell you as we walk. I already have the ideal spot picked out."

Gently he took her arm, leading her down the winding road toward the forest. "The first—and most basic—is good food. You have to admit that when you come right down to it, we're all pretty much slaves to our stomachs."

Miranda laughed, gesturing toward the wicker basket. "I see. And what goodies have you brought along to satisfy basic need number one?"

"Let's see. The menu for this afternoon includes a loaf of French bread, a hunk of cheese, some fruit, a bottle of mineral water . . . and for the grand finale, the most wonderful almond cookies in the world. They're dipped in chocolate."

"Everything sounds delicious."

"I hope you're hungry."

"Just hearing the menu is making my mouth water. What else?"

"The second basic human need is good music." Holding up the tape player, he said, "Mozart, Tchaikovsky, some Beethoven sonatas . . ."

"I had no idea you were a music lover."

"For me, music speaks to all the human emotions," he explained. "Capturing everything from anger, to sorrow, to . . . to love."

"I've always wanted to learn more about it," Miranda said, suddenly unable to look at him.

"I'd be happy to teach you," he said softly. They were both silent for a moment before Garth said, "Now, the third basic human need is physical comfort." This time he gestured toward the flannel blanket. "I chose this particular model because it's soft and warm. Besides, I heard a rumor that ants hate the color red."

Smiling, Miranda said, "That's one rumor

I hope turns out to be true." She thought for a moment, then, cocking her head to one side, said, "I thought you said there were four basic human needs. But you've only brought what we'll need for three of them."

He stopped walking then, letting go of her arm. Instead, he reached over to brush a lock of hair out of her eyes.

"The fourth," Garth said in a soft, tender voice, "is good company. And that, Miranda, is the most important of all."

Standing so still she was hardly breathing, Miranda looked into his eyes for what seemed a very long time. And then, afraid she'd get lost in their clear blue depths, she forced herself to look away. She began walking once again, glad that her dark wavy mane fell forward and veiled her face.

Just as he'd promised, the spot he had chosen was indeed the ideal place for a picnic. They came upon it unexpectedly after they'd walked through the woods, with Garth leading the way. It was a small clearing, almost a perfect circle, surrounded by aromatic evergreens and full bushes. Soft grass carpeted the forest floor, strewn with dried leaves in the bright hues of autumn. Through the center of the clear patch ran a brook, its water clear and bubbling. As it danced over the large gray stones that dotted its path, it created a sort of music all its own.

"This is beautiful!" Miranda exclaimed, perching on a huge rock at the edge of the brook. Ribbons of rich green moss ran over it, forming a delicate pattern. She threw back her head, inhaling the fresh, fragrant air of the forest. "Oh, Garth. What a wonderful spot! I've been exploring these woods ever since I was a little girl, and I don't remember having ever come across this clearing before."

He shrugged. "I've come to know this forest fairly well in the short time I've been living around here."

Garth set the basket down on the grass, then began unfolding the blanket.

"Can I help?" Miranda offered.

"No, thanks. Your job for the afternoon is simply to enjoy yourself."

Miranda was struck by his chivalry. Bobby had never treated her this way. . . . Quickly she banished all thoughts of him from her mind. Being with Garth was so exhilarating that the last thing she wanted to do was think about some other boy—even Bobby McCann.

Instead, she concentrated on how much she appreciated the chance to rest after the long walk, first through hilly Overlook, then across the uneven terrain of the forest. She watched as Garth paused to take off his jacket. Underneath, he wore only a T-shirt, drawn taut against his massive shoulders. He leaned forward, spreading the blanket out across the flattest part of the clearing.

Miranda continued to study him, noting how the powerful muscles in his back and arms rippled with each movement. His shoulders were exeptionally broad, his hands strong and capable. Drops of gold glinted off his hair as he moved in and out of the sunlight. She loved watching him. There was a sort of grace about him, an easiness with his body. An odd sensation stirred deep inside her. Once again she found herself wondering what it would feel like to touch him.

It would be so simple, she thought dreamily. To reach out, to rest the palm of my hand against his cheek, to brush my fingers against his shoulder . . .

"Hungry?" he asked, glancing back at her over his shoulder.

Miranda lowered her eyes. "A little. That long walk helped me work up an appetite."

"I'll have everything ready in no time."

"At least let me help you unpack," Miranda said.

A few minutes later, with a lilting Mozart sonata playing softly in the background, Miranda and Garth sat cross-legged on opposite sides of the blanket. The food he had brought was spread out between them. It wasn't long before her initial shyness gave way to talkativeness. It was easy, since he asked her one question after another about herself. He seemed sincerely interested in learning all about her studies and her life in Overlook.

Yet even as she spoke, finding him an attentive listener, she was struck by the one-sidedness of their conversation. She was revealing so much about herself, yet Garth remained the mystery he had been all along. Every time she tried to steer the conversation toward his background, his life in Portland, the aspects of his life about which he was passionate, he gave only the vaguest of answers. And then, immediately afterward, he came up with one more question for her to answer—invariably one that demanded a long and complicated response, once again placing her in the spotlight.

Finally he asked her something simple.

"Tell me honestly, now," he said, breaking

off a piece of one of the almond cookies he'd brought and handing it to her. "Isn't this the best dessert you've ever had in your life?"

She had to agree. "What about you?"

"Definitely. These are my favorites."

"Do you realize," she said slowly, her gaze traveling toward the gurgling water of the brook a few yards away, "that's the first direct answer you've given me all afternoon?"

She could sense a change in the air. Instantly she regretted having said anything. Miranda glanced over at him and saw that Garth looked stricken.

"I—I don't like to talk about myself," he stammered. "I suppose it's silly to be so shy—"

"I'm sorry. I didn't mean to be critical. And I certainly wasn't trying to pry."

"It's all right." Already his expression was softening. "It's just that . . ."

The tape they'd been listening to ended at that moment, leaving a dead silence hovering in the air. Abruptly Garth leaped to his feet.

"I'd better change that. Do you like Bach? I hope I remembered to bring along that one along. It includes some of his most famous contatas. . . ."

As he searched through the stack of tapes,

frowning in concentration, Miranda bit her lip. She was afraid she had offended him. She had certainly destroyed the magical mood that for most of the afternoon had encircled them like a wonderful protective bubble, a bubble that separated them from the rest of the world.

Glancing at her watch, Miranda was astonished to see that almost two hours had passed. The sun was dipping low in the sky, casting long, dark blue shadows over the forest. There was suddenly a chill in the air. It was growing late.

Regret descended over her like the curtain at the end of a play. She didn't want this day to end. It was too magnificent, too glorious. Just being with Garth, sitting together and talking, made her feel wonderful. She was amazed at how easily she'd opened up to him. How quickly she'd trusted him. Telling him so much, eagerly unfolding the layers of herself so that he could get to know her.

"I guess I didn't bring the Bach tape along," he said apologetically.

"It's just as well. We should probably get going. It's getting awfully late, and it'll be dark soon."

With a sigh, Miranda stood up, brushing

leaves and bits of grass from her lap. She stumbled as she suddenly lost her balance. It was only a moment before she felt his strong hands clasping her arms, keeping her from slipping.

"Close call! Are you all right?" His voice was thick with concern.

They were standing face to face, Garth still holding on to her.

"I'm fine. It's just that I was sitting so long—"

"My fault, I'm afraid."

"Oh, no! I enjoyed it!"

"Did you really?"

Looking into his face, so close to hers, Miranda could only nod. Suddenly he let go of her, dropping his arms to his sides and looking away.

"I'll walk you home," he said.

Their conversation was slightly strained as they made their way home. Miranda told herself it was simply because they were both tired after a long afternoon outdoors, breathing in the fresh clear forest air.

If only I understood him better, she thought. I wish I could read his mind. I would love to hear his thoughts, to feel what he feels. . . .

It was frustrating, not knowing what was really going on in this enigmatic young man's mind. At the bottom of her frustration was a very real fear. The fear that she had inadvertently said something or done something to drive him away. Once again she reminded herself that she hardly knew Garth Gautier. There was still so much she had to learn about him, so much she had to comprehend. . . .

But it wasn't her intellect that was wrestling with this fear. It was something that went deeper, into her very soul. It was that part of her that knew, instinctively, that she now had something extremely precious to lose.

CHAPTER
9

The evening of the dance was chilly, the approaching winter already a presence. As Miranda came into her bedroom to get dressed right after dinner, she rushed over to close the window. An especially icy gust of wind blew into the room before she had a chance to shut out the night. She wrapped her arms around herself and shivered.

Still, the sky was particularly bright, she noted, glancing upward. Through the window, she could see a round disk of a moon, glowing with yellow-white light. It appeared to be casting a cold, mocking smile down upon the world. In fact, if she cocked her head at a certain angle, it looked as if it were looking directly at her.

She shivered again, and then turned away, already thinking about the evening ahead. All day she'd been dreaming about going to the dance with Garth. She imagined feeling the strength of his arms around her and the warmth of his breath against her cheek as they moved together in time to the music. Leaning against the dresser, Miranda closed her eyes. She could practically feel his lips upon hers. She imagined putting her arms around his neck, pulling him close against her, feeling the heat of his body. . . .

She snapped her eyes open. In the mirror, she could see that her cheeks were flushed.

Miranda sighed deeply. What was it about him that had her so captivated? she wondered, her gaze still locked on her reflection in the mirror. She picked up a hairbrush and began pulling it slowly through her hair. She'd spent only an afternoon with him, seen him on only three different occasions, yet something about him created in her a remarkable feeling of exhilaration.

The truth was that she hardly knew him. She knew no details about him . . . what his favorite color was and what kind of books he liked and how many brothers and sisters he had. Yet none of that seemed to matter. Her connection to Garth seemed to exist on a higher plane. She couldn't explain it, but she sensed something powerful about him—and about the two of them together.

Perhaps they simply belonged together, she mused, dreamily watching the red highlights of her hair glinting in the bright moonlight. Maybe some force greater than themselves had not only led them to each other, but perhaps had even created each of them to be the necessary complement to the other. . . .

"Enough!" Miranda cried, laughing at how easily she was getting carried away. "We won't even be spending this evening together, much less the rest of our lives, if I don't get dressed!"

She took one of her favorite dresses, a deep shade of blue, out of the closet. As she pulled it on over her head, Miranda happened to catch sight of the gold box, displayed on a shelf in one corner of the bedroom. She experienced a pang of regret over her admirer's insistence upon remaining anonymous. Still, she thanked him silently as she remembered that it was his interest in her that had given her the confidence to invite Garth to the dance.

The finishing touch was a few pieces of

Native American jewelry she'd bought years earlier at a local fair. She put on a pair of silver earrings inscribed in black with an odd geometric pattern she'd always found intriguing. Then came a bracelet decorated in the same pattern.

Last came the necklace. Hanging from a delicate silver chain were tiny animals, carved from stones of different colors. There was a pearl-white eagle, a dark pink whale, a pale blue owl, and a lavender-gray frog. In the center was her favorite: a wolf, made from a black stone with swirls of murky green, the colors of the ocean on a stormy day.

When she'd finished, Miranda stood in front of the mirror once again, this time surveying her reflection anxiously. But even her own critical eyes could find nothing to correct, nothing to adjust. Everything was perfect. Tonight, she felt like a princess.

"Miranda?" Her mother called up the stairs. "Honey, Garth is here."

She grabbed the small purse resting on the bed, took one more look in the mirror, and dashed toward the stairs. She realized then she was nervous, afraid she might disappoint Garth . . . or in some way break the spell. But as she paused at the landing and saw him standing below, gazing up at her, all her anxieties vanished. Instead, a peaceful feeling descended upon her.

He looked particularly handsome tonight. He was dressed in a dark suit, well-made and cut to fit his broad shoulders and muscular torso. He stood tall and proud. Yet she picked up on his uncertainty. She realized then that he, too, was nervous.

"Hello, Garth." She tried to keep her tone light.

"Hello, Miranda."

His piercing blue eyes never left her as she floated down the stairs. A small smile was playing at his lips. She longed to reached up and run her fingers through his thick tangle of blond hair.

"Honey, you look lovely," her mother said.

Miranda glanced at Garth, curious to see if he agreed. The look in his eyes told her more than words ever could.

"Shall we go?" he said, unable to hide how much he wanted to be alone with her.

Miranda put on her coat then reached for the front door, and as she opened it a cold gust of wind blasted through, its intensity even greater than it had been upstairs. Automatically she reached for Garth's arm, clutching it for warmth and protection. And then, braced against the bitter wind, she followed him out into the night.

As Miranda stood in the doorway, her arm still linked in Garth's, she glanced around admiringly, taking it all in. The decorating committee for the Homecoming Dance had worked a small miracle in the school gym.

Yards and yards of royal-blue fabric had been draped across the ceiling, separating the cavernous room from the brilliant flickering lights set up overhead. Through tiny holes in the fabric the light was shining through, creating the illusion of a thousand stars twinkling down benevolently on all who gathered below.

The rest of the gym had been converted into a pristine forest. While a large area of the floor had been left free for dancing, a soft, fuzzy bed of moss covered the rest. Dozens of small trees and bushes lined the walls. There was even a small waterfall in one corner, next to the refreshment table, which was surrounded by a profusion of autumn flowers, chrysanthemums and other blossoms in vibrant shades of yellow, orange, and purple.

"Oh!" Miranda breathed as she and Garth stepped inside. "I had no idea what to expect. But this . . ."

"It is beautiful, isn't it?" He glanced around, taking it all in. "Almost like a real forest."

A good-sized crowd had already assembled, and the rock band was tuning up its electric guitars. The five musicians were perched on a stage that had been made to look like a hill by the papier-mâché rocks piled up around it.

"It looks like things are about to get underway," Miranda observed, leading him farther inside.

"Would you like something to drink?" he offered, gesturing toward the refreshment table.

She shook her head. "No. I'd rather dance."

Here in the midst of what seemed to her a primeval forest, she wanted to shut out the rest of the world, even among the throngs of students, to feel they were completely alone, together. As the two of them made their way toward the dance floor, she was longing to be close to him.

She was disappointed when the first few songs the band played were fast. Yet even standing a few feet away from him, moving together in time to the music, was exhilarating. It was as if they were finally a couple, paired off together in the midst of a crowd. She barely noticed anyone else, so intent was she on Garth.

Finally the band slowed down its beat, easing into a slow song. The dance floor thinned out quickly. Miranda glanced up at Garth, anxious to see what his reaction would be. Something in her melted when his face softened into a smile and, extending his arms toward her, he asked, "May I have this dance?"

Wrapped in his arms, sensing the heat of his body pressing tightly against hers, Miranda felt as if electric currents were running through her. It was as if a sort of energy was passing between them as she clung to him, half intoxicated, half fearful over the way in which she was being swept away, caught up in something over which she had no control.

"This is nice," she heard him say softly in her ear.

She tried to speak, but no words would come out. Instead, she simply nodded.

They danced in silence, their bodies echoing each other's rhythm, standing so closely together they were almost like one person. Miranda felt light-headed.

"This must feel strange to you," she finally said, trying to regain her balance. "Being back in high school, I mean."

"It is a little odd."

"What were you like in high school, Garth?" Miranda asked softly, looking up at him.

Garth paused a long time before speaking. "Let's just say I didn't have the most positive experience growing up." He paused before adding, "I've always been kind of an outsider."

"That's funny. I've always thought of myself the same way."

"You?" Garth's surprise was reflected in his tone.

"Oh, I've always been involved in a million activities. Committees, clubs, all that. But somehow I've never felt I was like everybody else. I always had this . . . this *yearning* to do something, oh, I don't know, something bigger than what everybody else settles for. Like there was more to life and I simply had to be part of it."

Miranda could feel herself blushing. "I guess that sounds kind of silly to you."

"No," he replied soberly. "It doesn't sound

silly at all." Miranda relaxed against him, reveling in the feeling of being completely safe in his arms. She rested her head against his shoulder.

"Miranda," he said in a hoarse voice, pulling away from her just a little.

"Yes?" She was almost afraid to look up into his eyes. Their faces were so close now, an inch or two away. His breath was warm on her cheek, his blue eyes locked onto hers.

"I know we haven't known each other very long. But I have this feeling about you. I've had it since the very first time I laid eyes on you. It's as if you and I . . ."

"I feel it, too," said Miranda, her voice nearly a whisper.

"There's so much I want to say to you. So many things. It's as if—"

It was then that he noticed her necklace. She could feel his entire body stiffen. "What's this?"

"I bought it at a craft fair. It was handcrafted by members of a local tribe." Studying his face, she could see the tension there. "Don't you like it?"

His expression softened. "Yes, of course I do. It's beautiful. It's just—I don't know, something came over me. I can't explain it. I'm sorry."

All of a sudden Miranda felt another dancer push against her back, nearly setting her off balance. It was Tommy Devlin, dancing with Selina.

"Sorry, Miranda," Tommy said.

"That's all right." Miranda smiled, then glanced over at Selina. "Hi."

"Hello, Miranda," she said. But Selina wasn't looking at her. Instead, her green eyes were narrowed as she studied Garth.

"Aren't you going to introduce me?"

Miranda cringed, afraid somehow that Selina would scare Garth away. "Selina, Tommy, this is Garth Gautier. He's . . . he's from Portland."

"Portland, huh?" Selina looked him up and down, then with a wink whispered to Miranda, "Not bad!"

"Hey, buddy. Good to meet you." Tommy was already whirling Selina across the floor. "Catch you later!"

"Friends of yours?" Garth asked.

Miranda had momentarily lost sight of Selina in the crowd. She finally saw that she'd abandoned Tommy and was instead huddled in a corner, conferring with Corinne. "I'm not sure."

The soft mood that had enveloped them

both just a few seconds earlier had vanished.

"I think I'm ready for something to drink now," she said.

Walking across the gym hand in hand with Garth, Miranda could feel curious glances bearing down on her. Envious ones, as well. She stood tall, proud to be seen with Garth. Still, she couldn't help feeling somewhat bothered by the intrusive stares. She felt as if she had to protect him from their prying looks, their whispered questions about the identity of Miranda Campbell's mystery date. She held on to his hand more tightly.

"What would you like?" he asked once they'd neared the table.

"Punch would be fine."

"Wait here." Garth cast her a quick smile, then disappeared into the crowd around the refreshments.

As she stood waiting, Miranda caught sight of Bobby. He was standing on the other side of the gym, among a crowd of his friends. Amy was next to him, talking to some other girls, punctuating her words by throwing her head back every so often and laughing a little too loudly.

Her arm was linked in Bobby's, yet he

barely seemed aware of her. Instead, his eyes were on Miranda.

Quickly she looked away.

Seeing Bobby reminded her of all the evenings just like this one that they'd spent together. But she wasn't with him tonight; she was with Garth. Bobby was part of her past.

Garth was already making his way toward her, two cups of punch in his hands. She smiled as he approached, glad he was coming back to her. The time for her to be with Bobby was over. Now, it was their turn.

"Will you excuse me a minute?" Miranda asked, lightly touching Garth's arm after a dance. "I see some of my friends over there. I'd like to go say hello."

"Of course." Garth smiled warmly. "I'll go get myself something to drink. Would you like anything?"

"No, thank you." After reluctantly letting go of him, Miranda made her way across the crowded gym floor. Three friends from her theater-arts class were standing together in the corner, chatting. She was anxious to catch up with them. Before she managed to reach them, however, she felt someone tug on her dress. Surprised, she turned around, finding herself standing face-to-face with Andy Swensen.

"Andy!" she cried. "What do you want?"

"I was wondering if you'd care to dance." He wore a big, sloppy grin, and there was a strange glint in his eyes. "That is, if your dance card's not already filled up."

"Thanks, but I'm here with somebody else."

"So I see." With his chin he gestured across the room toward the refreshments table. "So that's the poet, huh? He's the guy who turns you on?"

"Andy, please."

He leaned forward so that his face was next to hers. She could smell alcohol on his breath. All of a sudden a feeling of panic rose inside her.

"You could do better, Miranda," he went on. Now he was standing so close to her that he was almost leaning against her. "Come on, dance with me."

"Thanks, Andy, but I really have to go. I see some friends of mine over there and—"

"I guess what they say about you is true." He'd backed off, but his tone had become belligerent.

"What do you mean?"

"Oh, nothing much. Just that you're a snob. I tried not to believe it, but I guess they were right."

Miranda cast him a pleading look. "I'm not a snob, Andy. I just . . . please, I've got to go."

She started walking quickly, suddenly wanting nothing more than to get away. But she was in such a hurry that she didn't realize he'd grabbed her dress, taking hold of a fistful of fabric at the hip. Before she knew what was happening, she heard a loud ripping sound.

She stopped in her tracks, glancing down. There was a large tear in her dress. The silky white fabric of her slip showed through.

Andy laughed. "Sorry about that." The vague look in his bleary eyes told her he was anything but sorry.

"Andy, why . . . ?" She was trying desperately to remain calm, thinking to herself that she could pin it or that maybe somebody had brought a needle and thread.

He shrugged. "That's what you get for being so stuck-up."

He turned away, disappearing into the crowd. Miranda just stared, barely able to believe what had just happened.

Turning away, she once again made her way through the throngs of students enjoying the dance, this time moving toward the rest room. She only hoped that someone here had brought along some safety pins.

Maybe he's finally learned his lesson, she thought angrily. Even more, she hoped that from now on, Andy Swensen would leave her alone.

"You were right, Miranda. He's everything you promised."

Miranda turned away from the mirror above the sink in the washroom and saw Elinor standing at her side. Fortunately, one of the chaperons had thought to bring a needle and thread. A few quick stitches and her blue dress was once again presentable. She decided to forget the entire incident.

"You made it!" she cried, leaning over to give Elinor a quick hug. "I'm so glad you came. Are you having fun?"

Elinor nodded. "Asking Ricky to the dance was a brainstorm, Miranda. And he was so flattered!"

"I don't blame him. You look terrific." Miranda gave an approving nod at Elinor's dress, a soft pink that highlighted her fair coloring.

"Funny, that's exactly what Ricky said."

"Overlook's newest romance, huh?" Miranda teased.

"The newest, maybe. But certainly not the hottest. This place is positively buzzing about you and Garth! Everybody's dying to know all about your mystery man."

Miranda laughed. "Well, I'm going to keep them guessing for a long time."

"How long do I have to wait before I get to meet him?"

With a sweeping gesture, Miranda said, "Lead the way."

As she made her way back toward the dance floor, Elinor in tow, Miranda spotted Garth standing off to the side. His face lit up when he saw her.

"Garth, I'd like you to meet a friend of mine: Elinor Clay, Garth Gautier."

"Hello, Elinor." Garth smiled warmly.

"Hi, Garth. Pleased to meet you." Elinor cast Miranda a meaningful look, raising her eyebrows slightly to signify her approval.

"Ready for another dance?" Garth asked, turning toward Miranda, his strong arms already circling her waist.

She clung to him tightly, resting her head

against his shoulder as they moved to the slow, steady beat.

"I'm so glad you came down here from Portland," she said wistfully. "I hope you stay a long, long time."

"I'm certainly not going back there," he replied somberly.

His tone surprised her. "Why not?"

He continued moving in time to the music. "I got into some—well, let's just say things didn't work out for me there. I'm better off down here, in a place like Overlook."

"I'm glad you're staying." Miranda rested her head against his chest. "Then you'll still be here for the play."

"What play?"

"I auditioned for the lead in a play our community theater group is putting on. I won't hear the results for a few more days, but I've got my fingers crossed."

"I have a feeling you'll get it. What play is it?"

"*Saint Joan.*"

Abruptly he pulled away from her. She looked at him, startled. His blue eyes were ablaze.

"Let's go outside. I need some air."

It was crisp outside, although the wind had died down. Garth stood in silence, holding on to the chain link fence that separated the gym from the sports fields, his face lifted upward toward the moon.

"Did—did I say something wrong?" Miranda finally asked.

Her words brought him back to the present. "Oh, no, Miranda! I just . . . it's only . . . There's so much I want to tell you. So much I want you to know!"

"There's time," she assured him, reaching over and taking his hand.

Suddenly he embraced her, his powerful arms surrounding her and pressing her body close against his. "I can't believe I've found you, Miranda," he whispered.

She reached her face up toward his and closed her eyes, expecting to feel his lips upon hers. She yearned for him to kiss her. There was a burning need rising up inside her. Only being with him, touching him, kissing him mattered. Everything else had ceased to exist.

And yet, even as she reached for him, she could feel him drawing away. She could feel his muscles tense up; even more, she could sense some barrier deep within him, keeping them apart.

"Garth?" She opened her eyes. There was

a faraway look on his face, as if he were no longer with her. No longer in the moment. "Garth, are you all right?"

And then, wordlessly, he dropped his arms to his sides. She felt a rush of coldness. She knew it was a gust of wind, yet it could have emanated from him. She watched, feeling the distance between them grow.

"What is it?" she asked.

Instead of answering, he started moving away from her.

"Garth, please!" she cried, her voice pleading. "Come back! You can talk to me! Whatever it is, you can tell me!"

But it was too late. Already he was running away from her, across the field toward the woods. She was left standing alone. "Garth!" she cried one more time. But this time, there was no one to hear.

CHAPTER
10

He was aware of the sound of a voice. A sweet voice, edged with fear and pain.

"Garth?" he heard it calling. "Garth, are you all right?"

But it sounded so far away. And then even that was gone. He was aware only of the impulse to get away.

It was starting as it always did, with a tingling sensation. As the moon rose high in the dark autumn sky, his skin began prickling, fire spurting out of every pore.

He tensed up, his initial instinct to stay and fight. Yet as he glanced behind him, he could see through the open door of the gym that already the colors were fading. Far away drifted the faces, the walls, the bobbing balloons, and crêpe-paper streamers.

He saw only the light. It was overpowering. Bright surges attacked him. They penetrated his very being, invaded his soul. It was only a matter of seconds before his senses grew dramatically more acute. His nose twitched, picking up the subtlest of scents. His hearing also grew sharper, magnified hundreds of times. His head was filled with the buzzing of the tiniest of insects. The cracking of a twig falling off a tree a few hundred yards away. Even the sound of his own blood pumping furiously through his body.

The woods. He had to get to the woods. That was where he belonged now. The forest called to him, beckoning, its lure irresistible.

Hurrying across the field, he could feel the increased power of his legs. His muscles bulged, his stride lengthened. He was only walking, yet he could tell he traveled more quickly than the fastest human runner ever could.

By the time he reached the forest, the change was consuming him. He pulled off his clothes, dropping them at the forest's edge.

The urge to resist was completely gone. Gladly he succumbed. The process of shape-shifting was familiar by now. Inevitable. He experienced a sort of relief as he surrendered, giving in to what he knew he could not conquer.

Shrouded by the dense growth of trees, he watched as his arms stretched longer and thicker—until they were no longer arms, but legs. Golden hairs sprouted over them, reflecting the pale light of the full moon. His fingernails became elongated. Thick and pointed, they reshaped into claws.

His mouth ached as sharp white teeth pushed through his gums. His jaw lengthened, growing quickly as the teeth sprouted one by one. Even that pain was familiar, as familiar as the new shape and power of his now gigantic jaws. Still, he let out a howl, hearing his own voice and recognizing that this was not the sound of a human. The boy Garth was gone. The memory of him faded as the mighty beast, sleek and strong, dropped to all fours.

The beast could hear its own panting. Deep, eager, demonstrating its excitement, its readiness for the hunt. Its four legs radiated power and energy. They longed to run, to cross the forest floor in great strides, paws falling soundlessly on rocks and twigs.

Its hearing was by now supernaturally

strong. It heard a rabbit scurrying under some bushes, nearly half a mile away. Its nose twitched, picking up the enticing scent. Already its mouth was watering.

It let out another howl, listening to it echo through the valley. The tall trees seemed to shudder; perhaps they were only swaying in response to its heavy tread. For this beast was larger than an ordinary wolf, its strength and its size exaggerated beyond that of any other. As it raced through the forest, zeroing in on the rabbit that would be its first kill of the night, the werewolf was king.

It stood panting over the lifeless remains of the rabbit, no longer interested now that it had eaten. The tiny animal had done little to satisfy its all-consuming hunger. Once again the beast longed to run, to continue the hunt. It raised its head, its ears pricked, its blue eyes alert. Without hesitation it bounded through the dense undergrowth of the forest.

A surge of joy lit up its entire being as it raced beneath the full moon. Free. Unfettered. It was filled with a sense of having finally come home. This was where it was meant to be.

It delighted in the surrounding sounds:

the steady rhythm of its own panting; the dull
thud of its paws, confidently striking the
ground. It relished the feeling of its powerful
jaws, its teeth so large and so sharp.

Such power! Such freedom! The beast ran
and ran, relishing its own strength, delighting
in the feeling that it would never tire. The
full moon overhead seem to infuse it with
endless energy, driving it on and on.

And then it picked up a distinctive scent,
far away.

It slowed down, finally coming to a stop. It
stood very still, its nose twitching, its ears
pointed upward.

It knew that scent well. It had smelled it
before. It followed the scent, traveling more
than a mile through the forest. It knew it was
going back the way it had come, closer to civilization, but that didn't matter. All that did
matter was the hunt . . . and the gnawing
hunger in its belly, the hunger that had to be
satisfied.

And then it spotted him. A boy, standing
at the edge of the woods. Alone. The werewolf crouched behind a tree, massive chest
heaving, eyes fixed on the lone figure.
Silently it watched.

A scraping sound, a flash of light. The

acrid smell of sulfur burned the lining of its nose. It studied the boy's movements as he brought the slender white cylinder to his lips. The other end glowed orange. Then smoke billowed out from the boy's mouth, causing the wolf to start.

Still, it sensed there was no real danger. The wolf crept closer. It sucked the scent of the boy into its lungs. The hunger was terrible by now. The rabbit it had eaten earlier was all but forgotten.

The werewolf hesitated. The boy looked so helpless. So weak. Something deep inside the beast urged it to resist. To turn and run. For a moment it wanted desperately to alter the course of events it instinctively knew lay ahead. The impulse was strong and it fought to emerge. In the end, it could not.

Overcome with a crushing feeling of defeat, it realized that it was being pulled by a terrifying force it could neither understand nor control. It was powerless, its own will subjugated by the will of the other.

Besides, *this boy was an enemy.* It could not explain it; it did not seek to explain it. It simply understood.

The beast waited a few seconds, then continued its stalking. Silent. Slow.

Now it was only a few yards away from the boy. His movements indicated he had no sense of the wolf's presence. No fear emanated from him. He tossed the white cylinder onto the forest floor, crushing it angrily beneath his foot. The burning smell was foul to the wolf, but it was dwarfed by a much stronger smell.

The smell of the boy. Of prey.

A feeling of power surged through the wolf. A rush of energy, a tensing of muscles . . . In one fluid motion it headed toward the boy. Within seconds its powerful paws were upon his shoulders, pushing him to the ground.

"What the—" the boy cried out.

The wolf went straight for his neck. It bit down as hard as it could, feeling the strain of its jaws. Its sharp teeth sank into the boy's skin. With savage abandon it reached in more deeply, jaws working greedily.

It tore into the boy's neck again and again, then without hesitating moved across to his shoulder. It felt as if it would never get its fill. Its hunger was so great, so out of control. . . .

Finally it was sated. A good portion of the flesh had been torn from the bones of its victim. The fur around the wolf's mouth was damp and matted. Its blue eyes, glowing victoriously in the night, were ringed with red. Still, it experienced no relief, no joy.

Sitting beside its prey, it looked up at the dark sky, seeking out the moon. The perfectly round disk, shining like white gold, brought it little comfort. Throwing back its head, it let out a howl, so loud and so plaintive that it cut through the night like loneliness itself.

CHAPTER
11

By the time Miranda returned to the dance alone, the gym was nearly empty. The sight of the couples who still lingered, eyes shining as they danced together, was too much. When she learned that Elinor and Ricky had left long before, she headed for the Clays' house. It was late, but she hoped Elinor would still be awake.

Sure enough, the lights inside the Clays' house shone brightly through the windows. Miranda rang the bell, hoping Elinor's parents would be forgiving about the lateness of the hour.

She was relieved when Elinor answered the door, still dressed in her clothes from the dance. She peered out, bewildered.

"Miranda! What's wrong?"

"Oh, Elinor! This has been the worst night of my entire life!"

Elinor opened the door wider. "Come in."

Once Elinor's bedroom door was closed and the two girls were alone, Miranda let out a wail.

"I ruined it! I don't know what I did, but somehow I ruined it."

"Ruined *what*?"

"My date with Garth."

Elinor perched on the edge of her bed, gesturing for Miranda to take a seat on the rocking chair in the corner. "Tell me what happened."

Miranda accepted the tissue Elinor handed her. "Oh, Elinor, the entire evening was magic! Garth and I, dancing under the stars, feeling his warm arms around me, his body close to mine . . ."

Through her tears, Miranda smiled. "It was magnificent. I've never been as attracted to any boy as I am to Garth. I thought he felt it, too. There's almost something mystical about it, something I can't explain. . . ."

"It doesn't sound like a disaster to me."

"Wait! Then we went outside, and I could almost swear he was about to kiss me. And then . . . and then . . . he just ran off."

"Ran off? What do you mean?"

"I mean, all of a sudden he took off, for absolutely no reason. Across the schoolyard, toward the woods. I don't know what I did, or what I said, but . . ." Miranda stared down at her lap, her eyes puffy and her nose red.

"Oh, Miranda! No wonder you're upset." Elinor gazed off, bewildered.

"It was so odd. He got so . . . so distant. Something just came over him. And the next thing I knew . . ."

Elinor leaned forward and spoke in a soft voice. "Know what I think?"

"W-what?"

"That he just got scared and that within twenty-four hours, Garth's going to be on your doorstep, falling all over himself. Explaining. Apologizing. Begging you to forgive him—and to take him back."

"Do you really think so?"

"Sure. It sounds as if he really likes you. If you were having such a good time at the dance, I'd bet anything he was too."

"But why would he act so strangely? Running off suddenly like that. What was that all about?" She wasn't only hurt, she was angry. Part of her felt she'd be better off if she never laid eyes on him again. She was

troubled by what she had come to think of
Garth's dark side—silent, brooding, and distant—that somehow kept them apart. "'We
can never be,'" she said out loud, remembering the last poem she'd gotten from her
secret admirer. It seemed as if the same
words applied to her relationship with
Garth.

"What's that from?" Elinor asked, curious.

"I have a secret admirer." Miranda's attempt at keeping her tone light failed.
"Someone who leaves me poems—without
signing them."

"Poems?"

"Love poems. And presents. Once he left a
bouquet of wildflowers on my back steps.
Another time he left a beautiful gold box,
covered with jewels, in my bicycle basket."

"Do you have any clues about who he is?"

"No. It's a complete mystery. For some
reason, he thinks he has to keep his identity a
secret. He wrote one poem about a love that
could never be."

"Maybe he thinks he's not good enough
for you." Elinor frowned. "I'll bet he's a ju-
nior. Or maybe a sophomore."

Miranda hadn't thought of that. "Do you
think so? I'd been picturing him as an older

man. Someone worldly, sophisticated . . ."

Elinor laughed. "I don't think there's anyone like that here in Overlook!"

"Well, whoever he is," Miranda said wistfully, "his attention makes me feel special. And the way things are going lately, that counts for something."

Elinor handed her the telephone.

"What's this for?"

"To call your mom."

"Why?"

"To tell her you're sleeping over. It's close to midnight already, Miranda."

"Thanks, Elinor. You're great," Miranda said as she reached for the phone.

"Thanks for everything, Elinor," Miranda said after breakfast the next morning. Her blue dress was folded inside a shopping bag Elinor had given her, and she was wearing Elinor's jeans and sweater. Only her shoes were her own—those and her silver jewelry.

As she stepped outside on the front porch, Miranda paused. It was early, just past seven, and the sun was still low, barely rising above the jagged peaks of the Cascade Mountains. The leaves were the color of fire, and the air was cool, damp from the morning mist that was just now beginning to burn off. She reached up and stretched, took one more look at the clear morning sky, then bent down to pick up the bag.

As she did, a small piece of paper caught her eye. It was perched on the railing of the Clays' front porch. Written neatly on the front was: For Miranda.

Her secret admirer, whoever he was, knew she'd spent the night at Elinor's. He had to have followed her. As she'd walked through Overlook late at night, alone, shrouded by a thick blackness lit up only by the pale light of a full moon, he must have been right behind her. And then, when she'd gone into Elinor's house, he'd waited outside. He'd been watching. A shiver ran down Miranda's spine. She continued to stare at the envelope. Her usual reaction of feeling flattered was tempered this time with uneasiness. But after a moment's hesitation, she picked up the envelope, tore it open, and read the poem inside.

I've seen the fire in man's heart,
The ugly cruelty that lurks inside.
Their sticks and stones have torn apart

This flesh that longs to flee, to hide.

Yet all of that I'd rather bear
Than the misery, the torturous strain
Of knowing that sometime, somewhere
My own sweet love has endured pain.

It was a beautiful poem. But why couldn't its writer show himself? She stood on the porch for a long time, puzzling over what it all meant. Yet this time, just like every time before, there was no answer.

Miranda found herself heading toward the forest. Turning to the peacefulness of the towering cedars was the best way she knew to quiet the storm of powerful emotions whirling around inside.

As always, just stepping into the woods lifted her spirits. The thick white morning mist still hovered here. Branches leaped out of the fog at every turn, as if the forest were alive.

Miranda felt like the only person in the world. It was so quiet here, everything so untouched. In the forest, there was no sense of time. It could be the twentieth century, or it could be thousands of years earlier.

As she tromped through the woods,

Miranda let her mind drift, flitting like a butterfly, pausing in a hundred different places, yet lingering at none. For a moment she even forgot where she was. So she was startled when through the mist she made out a small, hunched figure standing alone in the woods.

"FeatherWoman?" Miranda said gently, not wanting to startle her.

Yet as the old woman glanced up, her jet-black eyes were filled with calm. It was as if she had known all along that Miranda would come. She might even have been waiting for her.

"Come closer, my child." FeatherWoman held out her hand, her gnarled fingers stretching toward Miranda. "I see that you, too, come to the forest when you are troubled."

FeatherWoman smiled, but her smile was somehow filled with sadness. "There is power in the forest. The power to heal, both the body and the soul."

"It does seem that way, doesn't it?" Miranda sat down on a rock, her arms wrapped around her knees. "I love the woods. It's so beautiful here. So peaceful. Coming here always makes me feel better."

She closed her eyes and took a deep breath, inhaling the damp freshness of the air. "Sometimes when I'm here I pretend it's another time, a much earlier time, back before there were towns like Overlook along the coast."

"The time when my people hunted in these forests." FeatherWoman closed her eyes. She spoke in a voice that was low but clear. "We built our settlements on the beaches, staying near the bays so we would be protected from storms. In the center was a Big House, the largest building of the settlement. It was used mainly for ceremonies. We used lime to whitewash it, then painted symbols of animals. Bright colors—red, blue, green, made even brighter by the contrast of bold strokes of black. And the totem poles were part of the building."

"What exactly is a totem?" Miranda's reluctance to interrupt FeatherWoman was overpowered by her desire to know.

"Totems are supernatural animal beings. They are part of each tribe's history. The members of each clan believe they are descended from a common ancestor, one who was tied to a supernatural being who had once appeared to him in animal form. That being gave him special powers, often the same powers that the animal possessed."

Suddenly FeatherWoman's eyes opened. The faraway look was gone. In its place was a hardness Miranda had never seen before.

"Here, of course, lived the Wolf Clan."

Miranda turned suddenly, having gotten the feeling someone—or something—was behind her. But it was only the trees, their leaves rustling in the wind.

"They are here." FeatherWoman's voice was hushed. "Can you feel their presence? Listen, Miranda. Give yourself up to them. They are trying to speak to you."

"Who? Who is trying to speak to me?"

"The narnauks. The spirits, Miranda. Can't you sense their power? They are all around us. In the rocks and in the trees. In the sun and in the moon. And in the animals.

"Listen and you will hear them. The whistling of the wind. The bubbling of the stream. The rustling of the leaves. These are their voices. That is how they speak to us."

"What are they saying?" Miranda's voice was edged with fear. She wanted to run, yet something held her back.

"They are sending a warning, Miranda."

"A warning? What are they warning you of?"

"Not me. You. They are sending a warning to you." FeatherWoman reached forward and grasped Miranda's wrists. The old woman's hands felt icy cold.

"Why? What's going to happen?"

"There are forces—strong forces, forces so powerful you cannot yet understand. They have chosen you, Miranda. You are in danger, terrible danger. Heed this warning. Prepare yourself for what is to come. You must listen to the spirits of the Wolf Clan."

"No!" Miranda broke loose from the woman's grasp. "No! I—I have to get away—"

Suddenly she felt a burning at her neck. She grabbed at her necklace, the silver one with the animal carvings. It was hot, she discovered, and the carving in the center, the wolf, was scorching her skin.

"No!" she cried again. She tore off the necklace, throwing it to the ground.

"Listen to the narnauks, Miranda. You cannot avoid your fate. The power of the wolf is the strongest of all the animals. There is much turmoil, a conflict between good and evil, and it is you they are calling to—"

"*No!*" Blindly Miranda turned away, running without knowing where she was going. She could feel their presence now. They were watching her, tugging at her, trying to pull her toward them. But she resisted. She had no sense of whether their power was good or evil; all she knew was that their strength terrified her. She had to run.

She didn't know how long or how far she ran, but Miranda suddenly found herself at the edge of the forest, where the growth of trees grew sparse. Up ahead was the main street of town. The black and white sign for Overlook Grocery was already in view.

Miranda stopped, her chest heaving. She felt light-headed, yet empty somehow. She took a few deep breaths. Things were getting back to normal. Her heart was no longer pounding quite as hard and the light-headedness was fading. The buildings of Overlook had replaced the shadows of the forest. It was over. Whatever it was, it had passed.

And then she glanced up at the totem pole. The carved head of the wolf was staring directly at her, its teeth bared and its eyes glowing red.

CHAPTER
12

He lay in bed, wide awake, tension hardening the muscles of his neck and shoulders. The sheets were a tangle at his feet, his pillow a rock. His senses were sharpened by the long hours in the dark, causing him to start at the slightest noise, the slightest movement, as if it were magnified a hundred times over.

The moon was waning. The night before, the time of the full moon, was already nothing more than a memory. Even so, there would be no sleep tonight.

The window to his left was open; the sheer white curtains billowed as a gust of wind came through, their tattered hems casting filigreed shadows on the wall. Yet instead of finding the coolness refreshing, Garth shivered.

The moon bathed his face in its beams. Even when he clamped his fists over his eyes, he could not escape its light.

It would not let him forget.

Desperately he tried to shut out the memory of the dance . . . and what had come after. Yet it persisted. The scene replayed in his head, so real it was as if he were living through it all over again.

Once again, he was there. In his mind he was running through the forest, tireless limbs pushing as hard as they could. He heard his own panting, felt the hot wet breath rising from his slackened jaws. His nose twitched in recognition of a familiar scent.

And then . . .

"No!"

Abruptly Garth sat up in bed. His bare chest was covered in sweat. Beads of perspiration trickled down his face, his shoulders, his back. He was struggling to find his footing back in consciousness, to tuck the memory away, to rid himself of it.

Make it turn out to have been just a dream, he pleaded silently. *Please, please . . . only a dream . . .*

But it hadn't been a dream. He could almost taste the blood, the flesh. He could feel the power of his jaws, greedily working to quell his terrible hunger. He could see the writhing of the boy's body, sense his agony . . . feel his terror.

He could smell death.

Garth leaped up. He glanced at the clock next to his bed. Three A.M. The night was creeping by slowly. He knew he could no longer lie in bed, overpowered by memories too excruciating to bear. He resigned himself to another endless night of roaming empty rooms, begging the long lonely hours to pass.

He had done this too many times before, he thought, as another nighttime trek began. Tonight, as he wandered through what seemed to him a prison, his loneliness was made even worse by his feelings of remorse . . . and his uncertainty over what would come next. He had killed. And now he would have to face the consequences. Just like in Portland, when the hateful powers in him had taken over, driving him to do what was so antithetical to his true nature. . . .

Just like the other time he had killed.

He willed himself to concentrate on something comforting. Miranda. A vision of her face came to him immediately. Serene, hopeful, gazing up at him and warming him with its beauty.

He remembered the rest.

When the light of dawn had first encroached upon the night, he'd retrieved his clothes from the edge of the forest. Overcome with fatigue, he shapeshifted back into human form, barely aware of the changes that swept over his body. Then, as always, he found himself standing in the dawn, half-dressed, blinking in the startling light of the sun.

He was exhausted. He could remember the exhilaration, the power, but it was all diminished by the terrible fatigue that engulfed him. He needed sleep.

Usually he headed for home, falling into a deep, comalike state for the rest of the day and the following night. This time, however, he could not. He knew there was something he had to do before he could allow himself to slip into that delicious oblivion.

He knew where she was. Her scent was already so familiar to him, so bewitching, that tracking her down was a simple matter. He found her quickly. She was in a house on the edge of town—not her own house, but the house of the girl he'd met at the dance. Elinor.

He'd written a poem, scratching it out on a piece of paper he'd found crumpled in his pocket, and left it for Miranda. He didn't expect her to understand, yet he had to tell her in his own way that he was aware of what he'd done. That he knew how he'd hurt her. And how knowing he'd hurt her made him hurt a thousand times more.

Now, instead of feeling strengthened by the gesture, he found it caused him even more agony. His frustration was so great that sleep was impossible.

If only he could explain to her! If only he could make her understand!

If only she could know him for what he was and still find it in her heart to love him.

Even attempting to imagine such an impossibility wrenched his heart. He needed to distract himself. And so he resumed his wandering, his aimless walking from room to room.

And then he opened the door to the ballroom.

A gasp escaped from his lips. He stood frozen, watching, unable to move his gaze from the grotesque vision before him.

There, in the middle of the marble floor, was a young woman. Her eyes were raised upward, her expression one of calm acceptance. Serenity. Perhaps even reverence. Her hair was cropped short, her clothes those of a soldier. She was tied to a wooden post, her hands bound tightly behind her.

At her feet was a bed of flames.

Joan of Arc. Being burned at the stake.

This time, the cry that escaped his lips was a plea for mercy.

There was none.

The flames leaped upward, higher and higher. The woman's sweet face was framed by black smoke, ugly billows growing thicker. The odious stench of burning flesh filled the room. The heat from the fire was so great he could feel it, even a hundred feet away.

He groaned, closing his eyes, wanting to shut out the horrifying sight. A nightmare, a voice deep inside assured him. It had to be a nightmare. It couldn't be reality. This couldn't be happening.

Cautiously he opened his eyes again, dreading what he might see, hoping that somehow the vision would have vanished. He saw the same scene. Only, this time the face had changed. It was no longer that of a young woman. Instead it was the face of a man.

There was no serenity in the man's face.

Only terror. Agony. Above all a desperate pleading, a supplication for mercy.

And then the scene grew fuller, more alive. Dozens of people—hundreds—filled the ballroom, anger and fear in their voices. They carried torches, bright orange flames leaping up and devouring the black of night.

From their midst arose what at first sounded like a chant. Louder and louder it grew, until finally he was able to make out what they were saying.

"Pierre Gautier. Pierre Gautier."

Something caught his eye. A little boy, standing on the edge of the crowd, clinging to his mother's skirt. The two of them looked on silently, their faces streaked with tears.

And then one angry voice, yelling out from the crowd: *"Tuez-lui! Tuez le loup-garou!"*

Garth repeated the words, his mouth so dry he could barely speak. *"Tuez-lui! Tuez le loup-garou."*

Instinctively he knew what they meant. *Kill him! Kill the werewolf!*

And then suddenly the face changed again. The bright light of the flames leaped higher, illuminating the features more strongly than ever.

The face of the man being burned at the stake was his own.

"No!" he cried.

He fell to the ground, his legs no longer capable of supporting him. His body shook convulsively. He could feel the flames covering him, lapping at him, singeing his flesh and inflicting the most excruciating of all pain upon him.

He cried out, again and again: "*Non! Non! Laissez-moi! Laissez-moi! Ayez la pitie!*"

Leave me alone! Have pity!

And then suddenly a stillness. Silence. Instead of the burning of flames, he began to feel the cold hardness of the marble floor. He smelled no fire, only the mustiness of the room. The shaking stopped, his fearful cries came to a halt.

Slowly, cautiously, he opened his eyes.

The vision was gone.

The room looked as it always did. The floor was unscarred. No smell of ash lingered in the air. There was only a terrible coldness.

He glanced at the row of windows that lined one entire wall and saw that a pair of French doors was open. Through them rushed frigid air.

He closed the French doors and locked them, and as he did, an odd feeling of peace settled over the room.

It was over. Yet the image remained, burned into his memory with such clarity that he knew he would never be able to banish it from his mind. He would continue to fear it, knowing that unless he could find a way to end his curse, this was his destiny.

CHAPTER
13

Miranda spent Sunday afternoon at her father's house. He'd seemed pleased that she'd ridden her bike over for a visit. Grateful, even. And it had been like old times, filling him in on the details of what had been happening in school.

The sun was low in the sky by the time she got home. As she leaned her bicycle against the garage and went into her house, she was suddenly struck by the fact that she now had two homes. That was going to take some getting used to.

"Hi, honey!" her mother greeted Miranda when she came into the kitchen. She was just finishing up a cup of coffee, and the crumbs from a piece of chocolate cake dotted a saucer. On the table was a bright handwoven place mat; Miranda noted that she'd even used a cloth napkin. Things were beginning to fall into place.

"I've got some great news," her mother said, looking excited.

"What?"

"Tyler Fleming called."

Miranda took a deep breath.

"You got the part. You've been picked to play Saint Joan!"

Miranda let out a loud squeal and threw her arms around her mother.

"The first rehearsal is tomorrow night. Seven thirty, sharp!"

"I can't believe it! Oh, Mom, this is the most exciting thing that's ever happened to me!"

"I'm so pleased for you, sweetie. I know how important this is to you."

Looking into her mother's eyes, she saw a light that had been missing for too long.

"Yes," Miranda agreed, giving her one more squeeze. "This *is* important."

Miranda sat in the third row of the theater, waiting for rehearsal to begin. The other actors were still arriving, greeting one another and chattering about the play. A few members of the stage crew were tromping around the stage, checking on the location of electrical outlets. A handful of lighting technicians fiddled with the spotlight.

She'd been so excited about this first rehearsal that the day had seemed endless. The only thing that made it go by any faster was the buzz around school that Andy Swensen had been missing since the dance.

"What *now?*" Miranda had wondered when she heard the news at lunch. Nothing about Andy would surprise her.

But all that was very far away. What mattered now was that in just a few more minutes, she'd be up on stage. As she sat waiting, she recited the first lines of Joan of Arc's opening speech, afraid of forgetting them.

Yet even in her nervous state, she knew that was unlikely. Ever since the night before, when she'd first learned she'd gotten the part, she'd been able to think about nothing but the play. She'd already begun studying more scenes, even bringing the script with her into the bathtub. Yet having to commit pages and pages of dialogue to memory was only the beginning. Beyond that, she was going to have to throw herself into the part, finding ways to make her character come alive.

Miranda was still marveling over the fact that she was part of a theatrical troupe of this caliber. It was difficult to imagine pulling everything together and actually putting on a play in only a few short weeks. She paused to calculate on her fingers exactly how much time there was between tonight and the first performance. Opening night was scheduled for a Sunday evening in November, only a few weeks away.

As she was agonizing over what a short time that was, she saw Elinor come striding into the auditorium, dressed in jeans and a sweatshirt, her cheeks flushed.

"Elinor!" she called, waving to get her attention.

The girl's face lit up and she waved back.

"Guess what!" Elinor cried, coming down the aisle toward Miranda. "I'm the assistant stage manager, apprentice to Carrie Billings!"

"Congratulations!" Miranda gave her a big hug. "You must be thrilled. I've heard Carrie is terrific. And the best part," Miranda went on, "is that when Tyler yells 'Take five,' you and I can hit that Coke machine together."

"It's a deal." Elinor glanced toward the stage. "I'd better run."

Miranda was about to settle back into her

seat when she felt someone touch her arm lightly.

"Excuse me. You're Miranda Campbell, aren't you?"

Standing at her side was an older woman. Her black hair, wildly streaked with gray, was cut very short, and a brightly colored scarf was tossed dramatically about her neck. "Yes, that's me."

"I'm Ann Stevens, the costume designer. Will you please come with me?"

Ann led Miranda to a backstage corner. A huge wooden desk—Ann Stevens's "office"—was covered with sketches, photographs, and fabric swatches. Strewn across the top were drawings of costumes for the play.

Ann shuffled through the sketches. "Here it is," she finally announced. "This is the suit of armor Joan wears during most of the play. I'll have to get your measurements for the tunic. You'll need gray tights and a pair of black leather boots to go with it."

Miranda experienced a wave of disappointment. "It's very . . . *official*-looking," she offered, trying to be polite.

Ann laughed. "Not the most glamorous costume in the world, is it? I think you'll like this one a lot better."

Delving down into the bottom of the pile, she retrieved one more drawing, a softly shaded watercolor. "This is the dress Joan wears in the first scene, when she first comes to the castle."

Miranda just stared. The dress was magnificent. Its lines were flowing and elegant, every detail adding up to create a dramatic effect. The bodice had long sleeves and a snug fit. It was cut low, off the shoulders, and the neckline was gently scalloped. The full-length skirt was cinched at the waist with an elaborately embroidered gold belt.

"Here's a swatch of the fabric I'll be using." Opening a drawer, Ann took out a square of rich red velvet. Miranda reached out and touched it, finding its lush pile impossibly soft.

"What do you think?" The costume designer was searching her face anxiously.

"It's beautiful! It's—it's the most gorgeous dress I've ever seen!"

Closing her eyes, Miranda tried to imagine what it would feel like to wear it. It would be magic, she decided.

Her reverie was ended abruptly by the sound of Tyler Fleming's voice.

"Let's get started!" he called, clapping

loudly from the front of the auditorium. "I want to begin with act one, scene one. Where are my actors? Where's my Joan?"

"That's me," Miranda cried. And she dashed off toward the stage.

CHAPTER
14

Tyler had asked that Miranda stay a little later to discuss the role of Saint Joan, so by the time her rehearsal ended—at almost eleven o'clock—Miranda felt both euphoric and exhausted. Everyone else had left earlier, and Tyler had stayed to go over his notes, so when she emerged from the theater she was alone.

The brisk autumn night instantly engulfed her. The sky was dark, its deep-blue color swallowing up the pale light of the waning moon and the few visible stars. The air was icy, stinging her face and hands. Everywhere there was silence.

Miranda shivered, caught off guard by the chill in the air. Still, as she walked alone down the path leading away from the Overlook Playhouse, she quickly became absorbed in thinking about the play.

What an experience it had been, being up on stage! She had tried on the spirit of a brave seventeen-year-old girl as if it were a garment, and the exhilaration had nearly taken her breath away.

Suddenly she heard a noise behind her. She turned abruptly. There was nothing. Deciding she'd simply imagined it, she continued on her way, proceeding more cautiously, keeping her eyes and ears on the alert.

But it wasn't long before she began to drop her guard, musing about the first scene, forgetting everything except the play.

And then she heard what sounded like a large animal in the brush.

"Who's there?" Miranda stood frozen on the path, her eyes darting about in a desperate attempt at seeing who—or what—was stalking her.

One of the dark shadows surrounding her suddenly shifted. Sensing danger, she automatically took a step backward. A voice deep inside was warning her, telling her to run. But somehow the connection between her brain and her legs had been severed. As in her nightmares, her feet felt rooted to the ground.

And then a familiar voice broke through her terror. "Miranda?"

A wave of relief washed over her. "Garth." As he stepped out onto the path, she brought her hands to her heart. "You scared me!" And suddenly she remembered the dance.

The hurt feelings rushed over her all over again. With them came the urge to protect herself. "I—I'm not sure I have anything to say to you."

"Please, Miranda. Give me a chance." He'd moved closer, grasping her arm. In the pale light of the night sky, she could see the pleading look in his blue eyes. "Give *us* a chance."

She turned away, knowing if she held on to his gaze she'd be powerless to resist.

"I—I don't know." She remembered sitting in Elinor's bedroom, sobbing . . . a part of her wishing she'd never set eyes on Garth Gautier again.

"Give me a chance, Miranda. I—I just want to explain, that's all."

She longed to throw her arms around him, to beg him to stay with her and never again leave her side. Yet her anger and confusion over his peculiar disappearance the night of the dance—the odd behavior she'd picked up on all along—continued to hold her back.

"At least let me walk you home."

"All right," she said softly, deciding there couldn't be any harm in that, and desperately wanting to be with him.

They walked together in awkward silence for a few minutes. It was Miranda who finally spoke. "Let's go through the woods. It's much shorter."

Miranda had never been in the forest so late at night before. She looked around, fascinated. It was terrifying in a way, with its dark unfathomable shadows. The trees, black silhouettes, looked like hands, their wiry fingers stretching toward her. Coils of mist wove through the branches, silently disappearing only to reappear somewhere else. Eerie, unidentifiable sounds pierced the night.

Still, she couldn't deny its beauty. The subtlety of the colors, pale grays and dark greens. The way the drops of moisture on the leaves caught the moonlight, shining like diamonds. The rich, intoxicating fragrance of the damp soil beneath her feet.

"What did you want to say to me?" she asked, once her eyes had adjusted to the woods' dim light.

He closed his eyes for a minute, then said helplessly, "I . . . I just had to get away."

"Away from the dance?" Miranda asked in a strained voice. "Or away from me?"

He looked as if he'd been struck.

"Please, Miranda," he said, his voice subdued. "Please understand and forgive me."

"Understand? Forgive you?" Miranda stopped in her tracks, turning to face him, the rage she'd been struggling to hold in suddenly springing to the surface. "What am I supposed to think, Garth? Here I thought you and I were . . . that we had something special between us—"

"We *do* have something special between us."

"Then why are you holding back from me? What are you hiding?"

His eyes reflected a deep hurt. "Miranda, all I can say is that, one day, I hope you'll come to accept me, even without understanding. I know that's a lot to ask, maybe more than any person has a right to ask for—"

"That's right, Garth. You have no right." Not wanting him to see the tears in her eyes, Miranda broke into a run. But she didn't get away fast enough to keep from hearing his final pronouncement.

"Faith, Miranda," she heard him call after her. "All I'm asking for is a little faith."

It was after she'd gone, run up ahead, that he felt his grip on the present suddenly fading, weakening, threatening to be torn from his grasp.

At first he thought it was being here in the woods, so soon after, that was responsible. The moment he had stepped into the forest and felt the rocky, uneven surface of its floor beneath his feet, inhaled the rich fragrance of the damp earth and the moldering leaves, he'd begun to feel strange.

Yet it was not the familiar tingling sensation of an impending shapeshift; it was something else. Something new. Something he couldn't identify.

But as he walked on through the darkened woods, he gradually understood.

He was not alone.

Someone—or something—was here in the woods with him. He could sense its presence.

"Miranda?" he cried, his voice hoarse. But already she was too far ahead to hear.

The air grew thick as a terrible feeling of doom washed over him, closing in on him, smothering him.

And then suddenly he felt a hundred hands grabbing at him, shoving him, clutching him, wrapping around his wrists. A thousand fingers snatched at him, nails ragged and sharp, flesh icy cold. He closed his eyes against their attack, blindly flailing about in a futile attempt at pushing them away. Yet when he opened his eyes, he saw no one.

It stopped. He waited. And then, through the billows of gray-white mist rising out of the trees, he heard a low, evil laugh. It rose up from the ground, a deep, cruel sound, resonating through the silent forest so that every branch, every blade of grass, trembled.

The sound was not human.

The air had grown still. It was foul, stagnant. Underlying it, growing in intensity, was another smell, something worse, something he knew was familiar but could not identify.

Slowly it came to him. It was the smell of fear. The smell of blood. The smell of death.

And then—a rush of cold air as whatever it was passed over him. He could feel its movement. Its very essence. *Evil.*

A low groan escaped his lips as the force

lingered over him, its grotesqueness overpowering and smothering him.

He was choking, scarcely able to breathe. He waited, each second an eternity. And then, as suddenly as it had come, it vanished.

The forest once again smelled fresh and damp.

It was over. Whatever had been here in the woods had finished with him.

For now.

Cautiously, he continued walking. Perhaps he had simply imagined it, he told himself. Maybe it had just been one of his dreams. Even though he'd felt he was sinking into a bed of quicksand, being dragged down into horrifying depths of something he was incapable of understanding, maybe, just maybe, it was nothing more than his imagination.

He took a few more steps, determined to regain his hold on the present. To find Miranda. He had to talk to her. He had to make her understand. He couldn't give up until he'd set it all right again.

And then he heard her scream.

"We just need to ask you a few questions," Officer DiSalvo said, concern underlying his gruff tone. "Can I get you anything first? A glass of water?"

Miranda shook her head, never taking her eyes off the clump of tissues in her hand. She shredded them again and again.

She still couldn't grasp all that had happened in the past hour. She and Garth had been walking home through the woods, Garth pleading for her forgiveness. She'd run ahead, stumbling into a clearing not far from the schoolyard.

It had taken a few seconds for it to register, but lying in the dirt—scarcely recognizable as a human figure—was a body. The face, however, was all too familiar, despite its look of frozen terror.

Andy Swensen.

"Miss? I asked you if you wanted to wait until your mother gets here."

Miranda shook her head. "No, I'm all right. Really."

"Okay, then. I'll leave you here with Officer Vale. She's going to take your statement."

Glancing up, she saw a woman police officer with a clipboard, bending over her and offering a kind smile. "You two really had a rough night, didn't you?"

Miranda realized then that Garth had been in the room all along. He was leaning against the wall right behind her. Despite their argument, knowing he was there with her gave Miranda strength.

"Let's go back to the beginning, okay?" Officer Vale sat down opposite Miranda at the long, bare table in the cheerless room. The walls were cinder blocks, painted a drab shade of yellow. There was no window, no clock, nothing at all to help soften the room's harsh edges.

Miranda took a deep breath. "I had just finished rehearsing for a play. I came out of the Playhouse—"

"What time was that?" The police officer glanced up from her notes.

"A little after eleven." She swallowed hard.

"Go on. You're doing fine."

"I'd started walking home when I found Garth waiting for me."

"Garth is your boyfriend?" Office Vale asked, gesturing toward him.

Miranda turned, her eyes locking onto his. She realized that neither of them knew the answer to that question.

"We're friends," she replied simply, turning back to the police officer. "Anyway, we were walking home and decided to take a shortcut through the woods."

Leaving out the part about the fight she'd had with Garth, she dug the fingernails of one hand into the flesh of the other and said, "The next thing I knew, I came across—" Her voice broke.

"You came across the body." Officer Vale supplied the words in a gentle voice. "Andy Swensen's body."

"Right." Miranda took a deep breath. "I knew right away it was him."

"He is—he *was*," the police officer corrected herself, "in one of your classes at school, right?"

Miranda nodded. "English. First period."

"Miranda, I know this is difficult, but did you notice anything at all unusual about the place where you found Andy's body? Think hard, now."

She did as she was told, closing her eyes so she could see it all again. The picture came to her easily enough; she doubted that she'd ever forget it. But there were no clues, nothing out of the ordinary.

"I'm sorry. I didn't notice anything except—except the body."

"Did you know Andy had been missing

since the night of the dance?"

"I'd heard something about it at school today." Miranda shrugged. "Andy was always getting into trouble. I didn't give it much thought."

"What exactly do you mean by 'always getting into trouble'?"

"Well, ever since elementary school, Andy's been kind of a bully. You know, picking on other kids, cutting up in class, getting into fights . . . just generally making a nuisance of himself."

Officer Vale leaned forward. "I'll be honest with you, Miranda. We've never seen a murder as grisly as this one in all of Overlook's history. There are signs of an animal attack, but the other factors don't quite add up."

Miranda blinked. "I don't understand."

"We'll have to wait for the medical examiner's report, of course, but given what we've seen so far, if it was an animal, its strength and the size of its jaws would make it like something out of a Godzilla movie."

The police officer shook her head. "There are no clear-cut answers, at least not at this point. For all we know, somebody brought some kind of beast up here that's not indige-

nous to these parts. Or maybe there's some
other way the perpetrator managed to make
it look as if Andy died from an animal maul-
ing."

Miranda shuddered, keeping her eyes
fixed on the edge of the table.

"As for the person responsible," Officer
Vale went on, "it's possible that he was a
stranger who didn't even know Andy. What's
much more likely is that this was an act of revenge."

She hesitated. "Think carefully now. Do
you know of anyone who might have wanted
to hurt Andy? Someone who had it out for
him—maybe one of those kids he picked a
fight with somewhere along the line?"

Miranda shook her head. "No. Andy was
annoying, but everybody basically accepted
him for what he was. We expected the worst
from him, and that's pretty much what we
always got. But I can't think of anybody
who'd . . . do that."

Officer Vale turned her attention to
Garth. "Is there anything you'd like to add?
Some little detail you knew about Andy?"

He shook his head. "Just as I told Officer
DiSalvo, I've never even met him."

With a nod of her head, the police officer

told them, "If you think of anything at all, call us. And thank you both for coming in."

Miranda was about to leave the room, Garth at her side, when she suddenly turned.

"Officer Vale?"

"Yes, Miranda?"

She hesitated. "Do you believe in the narnauks?"

"Narnauks?" Officer Vale repeated.

"They're spirits. The Native Americans from around here believe they're extremely powerful."

The policewoman cast her a quizzical look, as if she couldn't tell if Miranda were teasing. Then her face softened into a smile. Reaching over and giving Miranda's shoulder a squeeze, she said, "Go home and get yourselves a good night's sleep, both of you. And call us if you need us. That's what we're here for."

Miranda could hardly wait to get home. As for getting a good night's sleep, she doubted that was even a possibility.

As she walked home from the police station, the night felt cold and forbidding to Miranda. She pulled her jacket tightly around her. Garth, walking beside her in silence, reached over and slipped his arm over her shoulders.

"No, please." She moved away, not wanting him to touch her. "I—I just want to be alone right now."

"Don't you want me to walk you home?"

Miranda hesitated, then shook her head. "I'll be all right."

"Yes," Garth said, his voice distant. "I know you will."

They walked together another block, to where the road forked. One route lead to Miranda's house.

"Well, then," Garth said, keeping his eyes down, "I guess I'll say good night."

"Good night."

He was about to turn away when he suddenly stopped. "Miranda, I—"

"Tomorrow," she insisted. "Please, Garth. I just want to be alone."

She waited until he had gone, growing smaller and smaller as he walked briskly down the road that led to the outskirts of town, to Cedar Crest. As she watched him disappear, tears filled her eyes.

Never before had she felt so confused. The odd mixture of contradictory feelings that washed over her left her overwhelmed.

This had been one of worst nights of her life. Stumbling upon Andy's body that way . . . she would never forget the way he'd looked when she found him. Lying in the woods, so alone and so vulnerable. And his wounds . . . they were unspeakably horrible.

Then going to the police station. Being forced to relive the horror of the moment. The bright lights and the late hour had given the entire episode a surreal quality, making it seem like nothing more than a bad dream.

But it hadn't been a nightmare. It had been real. All of it.

Andy was dead. She was the one who found his body. Now she would have to live with that haunting reality for the rest of her life.

But there was something else dragging her down into a state of despair, as well. And that was Garth. She loved him; she knew that for certain. It was a feeling she'd never before experienced, yet now that it was flourishing in her heart, she knew it was love.

And yet there was a nagging uncertainty. It was always present. The feeling that there was something more to this brooding, mysterious boy. Another side to him, one he had yet to show to her but which she nevertheless sensed was very much a part of him.

She longed to trust him, to give herself to him totally with both her heart and her soul. Yet something was holding her back.

His odd behavior at the dance a few nights before only made her doubts stronger. She wanted to understand. Even more, she wanted to forgive. But that same feeling persisted, the feeling that he was hiding something from her.

Once he had vanished into the night, Miranda shook her head. This was no time to be agonizing over Garth and her bewildering relationship with him. What was even more pressing was her distress over Andy Swensen's death.

All of a sudden she knew what she was going to do. She had to go back. She had to return to the spot in the forest where she'd come across his body. Perhaps being there again would somehow help her come to grips with what had happened. Maybe standing there again would help her make sense of what seemed so senseless. . . .

It was dark in the forest. The full moon of three nights earlier was already on the wane, but the light it cast did little to illuminate the black shadows of night that were draped over the trees and rocks and hills.

Still, Miranda knew her way around the dense woods that surrounded her hometown. She belonged here. She'd grown up in their midst. And so she made her way through with confidence.

Even the sounds of the forest at night did not make her uncomfortable. They were all so familiar: the screech of an owl, the rustling of leaves. Tonight she felt at ease here among nature untamed, as if she, too, were part of it.

Besides, she was on a mission. She wanted to find the exact spot where she'd found Andy. With determination she made her way through the woods.

Sure enough; she found the spot. The police had encircled it with yellow tape immediately after removing the body, identifying it as the scene of a crime.

Had it been a crime? Miranda wondered. Was Andy murdered? Was he attacked by a wild animal? Or was it something else that had been responsible for the death of someone so young, something so out of the ordinary that even the police had yet to figure it out?

After stooping beneath the yellow tape, she stood next to the spot where Andy had been found. She wanted to feel something. Pain, sorrow . . . even relief. Instead, she felt only that same confusion.

None of it made sense. She had come here in an attempt at making the events of the evening come into focus, but to no avail. She could not grasp what had happened. It was simply too much for her to absorb.

She was about to turn away, to abandon the idea of coming to some sort of emotional resolution about what had happened, when she suddenly felt a gust of icy air. While the evening was brisk, this was a different sensation. A chill ran down her spine.

She knew immediately this wind was unnatural.

"Who's there?" The words came out in a whisper. She hadn't even realized she was about to speak, but all of a sudden the question was hovering in the forest, so strong it had a presence all its own.

Anxiously Miranda glanced around. She expected to see someone—or something. A shadow, perhaps, or the sudden movement of one of the trees.

She saw nothing.

She wasn't surprised. She'd known from the start that whatever was here in the forest with her was not visible. It could not be per-ceived in the way ordinary, earthly beings could be perceived.

And then it was all around her, as if its first tentative foray into her consciousness had burst forth, with no holds barred. It was everywhere. Icy fingers grabbed hold of her, the skin coarse, the jagged nails digging into her flesh. Her arms, her legs, even her neck resisted their grasp.

"No!" she cried, throwing back her head and closing her eyes. "Please, no! Leave me alone!"

And then a terrible sound erupted all around her, filling her ears, pounding through her throbbing head. Loud shrieks, cutting through the night with the sharpness of a razor. Howls, shrill cries that sounded as if they were coming from someone in terrible pain. In the background was a low rumbling sound, as deep and tremulous as thunder, yet so strong, so powerful, it seemed to cause the ground to shudder.

"This can't be happening!" Miranda cried. *"This can't be real!"*

There was no one to hear her. There was only the presence, still clutching at her.

A strange thought entered her mind:

They're satisfied. They wanted me . . . and now they have me.

She turned to run. Her only thought was that she had to get away. Yet the invisible hands still held on to her, their grasp firm, unrelenting. . . .

The hands were dragging her down. Pulling on her. Down, down, exerting strength she knew she could never resist.

"No!" Her cry was one of desperation. Even as it escaped her lips, she knew there would be no mercy.

They wanted me . . . and now they have me.

She sank to her knees, unable to resist their pull on her. She continued to struggle, knowing she could never triumph. They were too strong. Their power was too great.

Miranda was sobbing. She had lost her connection with what was going on. She knew only that she was being dragged further and further down, that her tormentor's joy grew with every passing second. . . .

And then suddenly she felt a release. One by one, the frigid fingers let go, their grasp weakening, their power lessening. No longer was she being pulled downward. No more were the ragged nails cutting into her skin.

They were letting her go.

Miranda raised her face upward. Through the darkness of the night shined a light. It was weak at first, so weak she thought she was simply imagining it. But it grew stronger and stronger until its presence was unmistakable.

"Save me!"

Her plea came out as a groan. She didn't know at whom it was directed. All she knew was that some other force, some other power, was also at work. Something positive, something good. And it was potent, at least as strong as the evil power that had tried with such determination to pull her into its ugly depths.

They were releasing her. In place of their downward pull was a wonderful feeling of lightness. Miranda's skin tingled, her face felt a flush of warmth. Her entire body was bathed in the welcome heat of the single beam that illuminated the forest.

And then they were gone. The evil presence fading as abruptly as it had come. The horrific noiscs had stopped, leaving in their wake an unnatural silence. A wonderful feeling rushed over her, a feeling that everything had been restored to the way it was meant to be.

She waited, expecting to find out who or

what was responsible for the ordeal she had just endured. Two such different experiences, one the worst feeling of her life, the other a relief so welcome that it transcended anything else she had ever encountered.

Miranda longed for answers. Yet as she stood alone in the dark forest, listening to the sounds of the night, she understood there would be none forthcoming.

Still, a magnificent feeling of tranquility lingered. She had come back to the forest, to the spot where Andy had met his fate, hoping to find answers. And while many questions still hovered, she had learned one lesson.

There had been more to Andy's death than a simple accident of fate.

There were strong forces present here in the forest. The narnauks. For the first time she understood what FeatherWoman had told her. Her tales of the good narnauks and the evil narnauks were more than folktales, quaint legends passed on through the ages.

The narnauks were real.

She had felt their presence. She had experienced their power. Miranda was now certain the Native Americans had not merely been spinning yarns, but that they had been relating their actual histories.

Even more, she knew that FeatherWoman's musings had been accurate.

"There is a terrible restlessness among the narnauks," she had told Miranda.

There had been more. She had started to make a prediction: "There's going to be—"

She hadn't had a chance to finish. And at the time, Miranda hadn't paid her much heed.

Now, remembering the old woman's words, a feeling of terror gripped her. Something was happening here, something beyond the realm of the here and now.

And for reasons she had yet to understand, in a way she could not comprehend, Miranda was part of it.

CHAPTER
15

A somber air hung over the First Presbyterian Church. Miranda took a seat in back, along with some other students from Overlook High who hadn't known Andy Swensen well. The altar was covered with bouquets and funeral wreaths. Organ music played softly in the background, not a hymn but a popular song. Miranda guessed it was one he'd particularly liked.

At least two hundred people had packed into the small building, their voices low and their expressions downcast as they settled into the wooden pews.

Even people who hadn't known Andy were distraught over the death of someone so young. And underlying everyone's shock was the unspoken question: Could it have been me?

Miranda picked Virginia Swensen out of the crowd right away. She was in the front pew, wearing a dark dress, her face half buried in the handkerchief clenched in her fist. Andy's father was at her side, looking lost.

Miranda's heart went out to them. What a terrible thing! To lose a son—and in such a violent way.

She continued scanning the crowd, this time searching for Garth. She wasn't surprised he hadn't come. Late Monday night, they'd parted on uncertain terms. Their disagreement over his behavior at the dance never had been settled; the trauma of finding Andy's body in the woods had been too great. As he'd walked her home, both of them were silent, their argument of an hour before suddenly unimportant.

Miranda's attention turned to the front of the sanctuary, where the minister of First Presbyterian, Reverend Parker, stood.

"I'd like to thank you for coming," he began in a halting voice. "I only wish it weren't such a sad occasion that was responsible for bringing us all together this morning."

He paused to take a deep breath, then

went on to talk about what a spirited and in-dependent boy Andy was. Miranda felt a rush of guilt as, instead of agreeing with Reverend Parker, she kept remembering what had hap-pened two weeks earlier. First Andy had de-liberately tripped over her feet in English class, belligerently accusing her of being re-sponsible. That same afternoon he'd snatched her poem, then used it to taunt her.

Two incidents in which Andy targeted her as the butt of his bullying, just two weeks ear-lier . . . and now he was dead. Killed in a grotesque way. Perhaps even murdered.

She forced herself to focus on the minis-ter's eulogy, to push out of her mind the no-tion that perhaps, somehow, all this had something to do with her.

After the memorial service, Miranda filed out of the church with everyone else. The Swensens stood by the front door with Reverend Parker, seemingly overwhelmed by a steady stream of people offering condo-lences.

Miranda's heart was pounding as her turn came up. A nagging feeling—that as crazy as it sounded she was somehow responsible for Andy's death—wouldn't stop haunting her.

"Mrs. Swensen? I'm Miranda Campbell."

The woman gave her an icy look. "I know who you are."

"I—I just wanted to say how sorry I am."

"Sorry? Sorry?" Mrs. Swensen's voice had grown shrill. "Andy had plenty to say about you, that's for sure."

Miranda's eyes widened. "But we hardly knew each other."

"Oh, really? Then why did you take such malicious pleasure in getting my boy in trouble?"

Taken aback, Miranda didn't know what else to do but turn away. She'd barely slipped back into the crowd edging its way out of the church when she felt someone touch her arm.

"Virginia's just upset," Mr. Swensen said in a kind voice. "She doesn't know what she's saying." He hesitated. "You're the girl who found Andy, aren't you?"

She nodded.

"That explains why Virginia is acting this way. I'm terribly sorry."

Miranda was relieved to leave the church and get back to school, where the students were just beginning to fill the corridors after the service. She headed toward her locker.

She had just opened it and was wresting

her English textbook from the bottom shelf when she felt someone standing behind her. She turned to see a face that was anything but friendly.

"Hello, Corinne," Miranda said dully, not in the mood for her friend's antics.

Selina wasn't far behind. "Miranda, Corinne and I thought we owed it to you to tell you the latest gossip."

"Selina, I'm really not inter—"

"It's *you* everybody's talking about," Selina said, her voice filled with mock concern.

"Actually, it's that new boyfriend of yours," Corinne added.

"You created quite a scene when you showed up with him at the Homecoming Dance," said Selina. "What a hunk! The whole school is buzzing about him. But nobody knows a thing about him . . . who he is, or where he came from. . . ."

"His name is Garth Gautier and he came from Portland!" Miranda said, indignant.

Corinne cast a knowing look at Selina. "That's what *he* says. Seriously, Miranda, some people think he might have had something to do with Andy's death."

"*Garth?*" Miranda cried. "That's outrageous!"

"He is a stranger, after all," Selina said matter-of-factly. "He just appeared from out of nowhere."

"You can't implicate him just because he doesn't come from around here!" Miranda exclaimed.

"It's not only that." Selina shrugged. "Nobody knows a thing about him." Her green eyes were steely as she added, "Nobody except you, of course."

Corinne leaned forward so that her face was close to Miranda's. "How well do you know this guy?"

"Well enough to know these rumors are crazy!"

"Maybe I should do some research on this Garth Gautier." There was a wicked glint in Corinne's blue eyes. "Or maybe even find out where he lives and pay him a little visit."

Miranda was as stunned by her friends' accusations as she was by the fact that people were talking about her—and Garth. The idea that he had anything to do with Andy's murder was preposterous.

Still, a disturbing image haunted her. Standing outside in the schoolyard the night of the dance, watching as Garth sprinted toward the woods, the same woods in which Andy's body had been found . . .

No! a voice inside cried. *Impossible!*

"I'd be careful if I were you, Miranda," Selina was saying. "You never know who'll be next."

"Thanks for your concern," Miranda said, slamming her locker shut and taking off, wanting nothing more than to get lost in the crowd quickly filling the corridor.

Out on the edge of Overlook, an air of desolation hung as thick as the mist that blanketed the forest. The pale late-afternoon sun was barely visible against the gray sky as Miranda struggled to maneuver her bike over the narrow dirt road, pitted and uneven from years of neglect.

Winding Way was treacherous, an endless path of sharp turns and unexpected twists that snaked up into the hills. All around were rotted fences, jutting out from fields of weeds. She hadn't been on this road since she was a child, when she and her girlfriends used to head out on their bikes in search of adventure. She was dismayed over its state of terrible disrepair. Yet what struck her most was the silence.

Nothing, not even birds, seemed to dwell here.

It was Garth who had compelled her to come here to the outskirts of town. She had to see him. The memorial service, Mrs. Swensen's sharp words, the terrible insinuations of Corinne and Selina . . . it had all been too much for her to bear alone. By the time the final bell rang, her desire to be with Garth had grown to a longing that was almost desperate.

She'd had no idea where he lived. She stopped in at the library, hoping that someone there might know.

"Now let me see," said Ms. Wallace, the library clerk. She'd retrieved a box of file cards from under the counter and shuffled through them, peering through her eyeglasses. "He did apply for a card recently, and so I should have— Oh, yes, here it is: Garth Gautier . . . Winding Way."

The library clerk frowned. "Hmmm. The only house I know of on Winding Way is that dilapidated old estate. What is it called? Cedar Crest?"

Miranda was startled. "Garth lives at Cedar Crest?"

"I doubt it. Nobody's inhabited that old

place for years. I'm surprised the Board of
Health hasn't had it leveled by now." Ms.
Wallace shook her head. "There must be
some mistake."

Something told Miranda there was no mistake. "Thanks anyway," she told the librarian,
and headed toward Winding Way.

Miranda had an even stronger sense that
she was on the right track when she rounded
the final bend in the road. There Cedar Crest
rose up suddenly from above the tall trees
that separated it from the rest of the world.
Ever since Miranda was a child, the house
had made her think of a European castle.
Made of stones that were a pale shade of gray,
its two imposing wings were joined by an awe-
inspiring tower.

Undoubtedly a showplace at one time, it
was now forbidding. Even in the bright afternoon light, it was shrouded in shadow. The
darkened windows resembled dozens of unseeing eyes. Miranda shivered.

She leaned her bicycle against a tree, then
cautiously made her way toward the front
door. Up close, she could see that the house
was in a terrible state of decay. Many of the
stones were pitted or even disintegrating, victims of decades of neglect. The brick path

leading from the circular driveway up to the front door was overgrown with weeds. She wondered if the crumbling steps would support her weight.

It was growing more and more difficult to believe that anyone lived here, but somehow, for Garth, it made sense. Miranda reached for the heavy brass knocker.

After a moment the door opened slowly and Garth peered out, his expression quickly changing from fear to astonishment.

"Miranda!" he gasped. "What are you doing here?"

"Can I come in?"

He hesitated for a moment, as if deciding, then stepped aside to let her in.

Relieved, Miranda walked into the foyer. It took a few seconds for her eyes to adjust. The interior of Cedar Crest was in the same state of decay as the exterior. She found herself in a huge entryway that led to a dramatic marble staircase edged by an intricately carved wooden banister. On either side of her were cavernous rooms.

Once, she could see, they'd been elegant. Now they contained barely any furniture; the few pieces that remained were obvious casualties of time. Piles of rubble were pushed into corners. Paint was peeling, decorative trim was faded. And everywhere there were shadows, as if there was not enough light in the entire world to bring this place alive again.

"You shouldn't have come," Garth said evenly. He was standing behind her as she surveyed the decrepit castle that was his home.

She quickly forgot all about her bizarre surroundings. "I had to see you," she explained, turning to him.

"You don't belong here," he said in the same monotone.

"Oh, Garth, just hold me!" Disregarding his coldness, she wrapped her arms around him. Clutching his shoulders, she gazed up at him. In his eyes she searched for the warmth, the acceptance she craved. She desperately needed him to tell her she wasn't alone.

A small eternity passed. And then finally she felt what she had yearned for for so long: he clasped his arms around her fiercely, drawing her close. She collapsed against his powerful chest, feeling a sense of safety, of security, that she couldn't remember having felt for a long time.

It was like coming home.

She raised her face to his. The intensity in his blue eyes created a stirring feeling deep inside her. And then he leaned forward, pressing his parted lips against hers. Gently at first, as tentatively as if he were asking a question. But his kiss quickly grew more ardent. Miranda was astonished by the fervor with which she responded. Eagerly she gave in to it. Reaching up, she encircled his neck with her arms, her body melting against his.

Finally he drew back, nuzzling her neck. "My sweet, sweet Miranda," he whispered, his breath hot against her skin.

"Hold me," she pleaded, clinging to him.

He grasped her even more tightly. "Oh, Miranda, what have they done to you?"

In a halting voice she told him everything. All about the memorial service for Andy Swensen. His mother's reaction to her expression of sympathy. Corinne and Selina's accusation. Even her own self-doubts, her suspicion that, in some way she couldn't explain, she'd had something to do with Andy's death.

"My poor Miranda." Garth embraced her in his muscular arms, holding her as if he could infuse her with some of his own strength. "Let's forget all that for now. Let's just appreciate this moment, right now."

He took her gently by the hand and led her through the house. Miranda was breathless as she took it all in. Room after room, each more beautiful, more ornate than the last . . . all of them slipping into ruin as if they'd been cursed. There was so much she wanted to know, yet she didn't dare ask. Instead she concentrated on Garth and the wonder of the two of them being together.

Out back was a garden. Miranda could tell that, like the rest of the house, it had once been an enchanted place. Now it was covered with weeds, the meandering paths barely visible through the stubby grass that pushed its way through. Still, she could make out what had once been a rose garden, picturing it in her mind as it must have looked in late spring, alive with pink and red and yellow buds. In one corner was a fish pond, an oddly shaped pool of water that was now murky and covered over with algae. Off in the distance was a maze, fashioned from shrubs that over time had become oddly misshapen.

Despite its state of decline, Miranda was

awestruck, and even a bit intimidated, by its grandeur.

"It's just magical!" she breathed, sinking onto a crumbling concrete bench. "How did you come to live here?"

"My family owns this estate. My great-grandfather built it after he made a fortune in the lumber industry." He glanced around with a rueful smile. "This was his reward."

"Where is he now?"

"He died a long time ago. His son, my grandfather, had already established himself up in Portland, so he just closed it up. When I had to . . . when I decided to leave Portland, I came down here and opened the place up."

"Isn't it lonely, living here by yourself?" Miranda asked with concern.

A startled look crossed Garth's face. Then, in an even voice, he told her, "I've been alone my whole life."

They sat together for a long time, hands locked together, enjoying the garden, allowing the peacefulness of the place to settle over them. Miranda found herself telling him so much of what was in her heart—the pain, the confusion, even the hope. Once again she was surprised by how easy it was being with him. Talking to him. Trusting him. Gradually a sense of calm returned.

"Let's go inside," he suggested when the sun began dipping in the sky and the autumn breezes grew stronger. He led her back into the house, this time going off in a different direction.

They ended up in the ballroom. Miranda let out a gasp. What a magnificent room! Her eyes traveled upward, taking in the hand-carved running frieze joining the walls to the ceiling, the elaborate gold-leaf trim, the ornate cornices above the windows.

"Oh, Garth, it's gorgeous," she cried, taking his arm. "This entire house is like something out of a dream. Wouldn't it be wonderful if together we could bring it alive again? Imagine! We could make it just as beautiful as it was when your great-grandfather first built it."

Miranda grew more excited as her fantasy continued. "I could work in the garden. I'll bet that in a single summer I could get it back into terrific shape. And inside, we could paint and make repairs. . . ."

She cast a sidelong glance at Garth, anxious to see if he was with her. Instead, the look on his face frightened her.

"What is it, Garth?"

"It's hearing you talk like that."

Miranda bit her lip. "I'm sorry. I didn't mean—"

"Don't you see, Miranda?" he cried. "Don't you know that's what I want, too? For us to be together? More than anything. I'd give anything if we could make it happen!"

"Why can't we?" Miranda said, undaunted by the force of his words.

"We can't see each other anymore," Garth said evenly. "You must accept that."

"All I understand is that I love you," she said in a quiet voice, "and I want to stay with you."

She took a step forward then, her eyes locked on his, saying with her body what she could never put into words. Holding her breath, she waited for his reply.

But instead of feeling him melt against her the way she'd hoped, she saw his muscles tense.

"No, Miranda. Don't."

"But I do love you! I can't just stop. I—I don't want to stop!"

Garth buried his face in his hands and paced about the room, talking more to himself than to Miranda. "I was afraid of this. I tried to stop it, I thought I could control it—"

"Garth, what is it? Why is it wrong for me to love you?"

"You don't understand." As Garth turned to face her, Miranda expected to see anger in his blue eyes. Instead, she saw desperation. "I'm not what you think I am."

"But Garth—"

"Go away, Miranda," he pleaded. "Before it's too late."

She reached up and gently placed her hand against his cheek. "It's already too late."

He moved her hand away. "Miranda, there are things about me you don't know."

"Then tell me," she pleaded in a tender voice. "I want to know. I want to know everything about you."

"You couldn't possibly understand—"

"I understand how I feel. I understand, for the first time in my life, what it means to be in love."

She moved toward him, but he stepped back. As he did, her frustration gave way to anger.

"You're right, Garth. I *don't* understand. I see that there could be something special, something wonderful between us. There already is— or at least I thought there was. But you're afraid of it. You're turning your back on it."

"Listen to me, Miranda! It's not what you think!"

"I don't know what to think. All I know is that you're sending me away. I'll go. You're not the only boy in the world who could possibly care for me."

"What are you talking about?"

A surge of power rushed through her as she said, unable to stop herself, "There's someone else. Someone who pours out his heart to me in beautiful love poems. Someone who's not afraid of my love!"

She whirled around, racing toward the door of the ballroom. As she did, she heard him say her name one more time.

"Miranda!" It came out like a groan, more a desperate plea than a cry.

She didn't turn back. Instead she rushed outside. The air was tinged with iciness. The approaching dusk was already painting the sky with reds and oranges, the towering trees darkening against the fiery backdrop.

Tonight Miranda found no comfort in her surroundings. Her pain was so wrenching that the dramatic landscape only served to heighten her feelings of loss and hopelessness.

CHAPTER
16

She was gone.

He stood at the window, watching her go. His world was spinning around him and he had nothing to grab on to. Through his head echoed the words he had spoken only minutes before. "We can't see each other anymore. You must accept that."

Yes, he had sent her away. Insisted that they never see each other again. It was he who had made it happen. It was his decision alone, rooted in his irrefutable belief that this was the way it had to be.

She'd wanted to stay. To try to understand.

He knew he could never make her understand.

Already her life had been tainted by his curse. The evil power that controlled him had led him to choose Andy Swensen as his victim, targeting him as an enemy.

Andy had been Miranda's enemy, not his.

She sensed she'd had something to do with Andy's death. She'd cried as she told him. And he felt as if his heart was being ripped into pieces.

He had caused Miranda pain.

He turned away from the window, no longer able to bear watching her fade from sight. As he did, he caught sight of a stack of books piled up near the door. Library books, the thick dusty tomes he had been poring over. For weeks he had dedicated himself to trying to find some explanation, a way of understanding the hateful curse he lived under. Desperately he'd tried to find answers.

There were none.

Frustration rose up inside him like a tidal wave. With all his strength he sent the books flying across the marble floor. "Somebody help me, please!" he cried, his body shaking. Yet he knew there was no help for him. He fell to the floor, sobbing as he hadn't since he was a child. Never in his life had he felt so alone.

When he finally stood, the sun was disappearing below the horizon. Deep shadows

were draped around the rooms. Darkness
had fallen.

Completely drained of energy, he stumbled to his bedroom, falling onto the bed. He
longed for the sleep that would release him,
knowing even as he wished for it that he
would not be so blessed.

Lying back, he stared at the ceiling, watching the shifting patterns of the tree branches.
He allowed himself to be hypnotized by the
motion, gradually feeling the tension in his
muscles lessen, the turmoil in his thoughts
grow more calm. . . .

He could feel himself slipping away, drifting toward another place. It was like being
sucked in by quicksand, being pulled downward, slowly but with certainty. He simply
gave in.

Around him, the walls of the room dissolved. The shadows on the ceiling trans-
formed into the actual branches of trees. The
moon, before shining through the window,
was now directly overhead, bright against a
backdrop of blackened sky.

It was a full moon.

Suddenly he was running through the forest, exhilarated over his own power. He relished all of it: the strength of his muscles, the

length of his limbs, the acuteness of all five of his senses.

He was no longer a man. The beast had returned.

Eagerly it succumbed to the thrill of racing over the underbrush, covering the ground in six-foot leaps. It reveled in the sensation of the damp, cold night air that surrounded it. The soft earth yielding easily beneath its formidable weight. The pungent smell of decaying leaves, rising from stagnant bogs.

Electrified by the challenge of the hunt, it headed toward civilization, ignoring the scent of the wild animals that scurried away, desperate to get out of the beast's path.

It knew what its prey would be.

Closer and closer toward civilization it traveled, anticipation rushing through every part of its body. This time, it was not the act of feeding it craved. It was the act of killing.

Suddenly it stopped. It knew its victim was near . . . but there was something else. The presence of others, many others. The flash of fire, rising out from a clearing. And the rhythmic pounding of drums, cutting through the night.

Yet it felt no fear as it continued on. It knew it was mightier than the others. Even if

all of them banded together, they would be
no match for it.

It possessed the power, the strongest
power of them all.

When it darted into the clearing, it saw
the terror in their faces. They ran from the
beast—their lean muscular bodies, glowing
like embers in the fire's intense light, fleeing into the forest. It barely glanced at
them. Instead it headed for one of the trian-
gular huts, painted all over with animal
shapes.

Painted with images of the wolf.

It stood outside the opening, wanting to
savor the moment. It could smell its prey.

The victim it had chosen was human. It
was their leader, the strongest member of
their tribe.

Inside the hut, on the verge of clamping
its jaws around the soft neck, delighting in
the irresistible . . .

No!

Garth suddenly snapped back to the present. He blinked, meanwhile struggling to
catch his breath, to quiet his pounding heart.
Once again he was in his room, surrounded
by four walls. Once again he was a man,
bathed in sweat, his limbs thrashing about, at-

tempting to free themselves from the damp tangle of sheets.

It was over. It hadn't been real at all. It had been nothing but a vision.

Yet this new vision left him in turmoil. What did it mean? The werewolf had been in the midst of a tribe of Native Americans, perhaps those who had once inhabited this very area. Was that another piece of the Gautiers' horrific past, the loathsome history that his curse forced him to continue?

As he was pondering this possibility, he realized he was not alone.

The presence of someone else—or something else—was unmistakable. He could feel it breathing, its hot, wet breath threatening to smother him, its heart throbbing with such vehemence the room was vibrating.

He knew without question that whatever it was, it was pure evil.

And then, the laughter. Rising up from the ground, as powerful as thunder.

He had heard it before. That night in the forest, right before Miranda had come across Andy's body.

This, he knew, was the power that controlled him.

"Get out!" he yelled. His hands were

clenched into tight fists, his face contorted in a grimace. He closed his eyes, digging down deep into his very soul, searching for the strength to banish it once and for all.

Yet even as his cry was swallowed up by the emptiness of the room, he knew instinctively it was stronger than one man could ever be.

An hour after she'd returned from Cedar Crest, Miranda lay stretched across the couch, staring at the first page of a thick novel, rereading the same sentence for the fifth time, yet still not grasping its meaning. Unable to concentrate on the words in front of her, she kept seeing two faces: hers and Garth's.

What did it mean, his secretiveness? Was whatever it was he was hiding really that terrible? What could be so horrible that he couldn't tell her, so unforgivable that it meant they had to stay apart?

The sudden ringing of the doorbell dragged her out of her reverie. From overhead came the sound of water rushing through pipes, a reminder that her mother was in the shower.

"Coming!" Miranda yelled, bounding off the couch.

Standing at the front door was a deliveryman, a long white box in his arms. Printed on top was the name Blossoms Florist.

He peered at a slip of paper he'd pulled from his pocket. "Miranda Campbell?"

"That's me."

He handed her the box. "Lucky girl. Looks like roses."

Eagerly Miranda pushed aside the countless folds of green tissue paper. Nestled inside she found a single perfect flower, a creamy white long-stemmed rose.

"How beautiful," she murmured, lovingly taking it out of the box.

She tore open the tiny white envelope she'd found tucked at the bottom of the box. There was a white sheet of paper folded up inside. Written on it was a poem.

> *Of all the words that ever pass*
> *On land or sea or sky,*
> *The saddest I now say to you,*
> *My heart's true love: Good-bye.*

Good-bye.

The word rang through her head. Whoever had written the poem had been right; it was the saddest word of all.

So sad that she couldn't accept it. Losing

Garth and then her secret admirer so close together left her feeling utterly abandoned. She couldn't let him go, not when the wrenching pain she was feeling threatened to consume her.

And now something else tugged at her. A new thought, one that had been hovering at the back of her mind for some time, was finally coming into focus.

She got on her bike, laying the creamy rose carefully in her wicker basket, and headed for Norton. The route was by now familiar, although this time it wasn't her father's house she was so intent on going to. It was Blossoms Florist.

The florist was on the corner; a hand-painted sign over the door spelled "Blossoms" with a chain of daisies.

She was about to go inside when the door opened. Miranda stepped back to let the other person pass, then started as she saw who it was.

"Hello, Amy." She tried to keep her tone friendly. "Small world."

"So it seems. I was just sending flowers to Bobby." A slow smile played at Amy's lips. "It's so unfair that boys are always the ones sending the flowers, don't you think?"

Miranda felt a twinge of jealousy, but then glanced down at the rose in her hand.

Amy's eyebrows shot up. "Looks like you've got a fan."

Miranda brought the rose up to her face, stroking her cheek with its soft petals. "Nice to see you, Amy."

Inside the flower shop, the delicate scents of a dozen different varieties of flowers co-mingled, creating an intoxicating perfume. The tiny store was bursting with colorful bouquets of carnations, chrysanthemums and asters. A black cat patrolled the shop, its long tail swaying lazily as it wove its way through the profusion of blossoms. Baroque chamber music played softly in the background.

A woman stood behind a small counter. Glancing up from the pile of invoices and catalogues, she asked, "May I help you?"

"Actually, I'm here for information," Miranda replied.

"Information?"

"Yes. This single white rose was just delivered to my house. The card wasn't signed."

The woman smiled. "You've got a secret admirer."

"Apparently. I'd like to find out who he is."

"Oh, dear." The woman's smile faded.

"I'm afraid we're not allowed to give out that information. Store policy."

"Couldn't you make an exception? Just this once?"

"I'm sorry, but—"

They were interrupted by a loud crash that caused Miranda to jump. The cat's flicking tail had knocked over a large vase, shattering it and sending the pieces flying. Mums were strewn all over the floor.

"Willie, get out of there!" the woman chided. Shooing away the cat, she crouched down and gingerly began picking up the shards.

"Can I help?" Miranda offered.

"Oh, would you? Get me one of those catalogues, over there on the counter. I'll put the pieces on it, since I don't have—Willie, get away! You'll cut your paw!"

Miranda was pulling a glossy florist-supply catalogue out from under the haphazard collection of invoices when she noticed a date book. The heading on top was yesterday's date. She cast a furtive glance at the woman and saw she was on her hands and knees, retrieving a sliver from underneath a display of gladiolus. Quickly Miranda scanned the list scrawled in the date book.

Written at the very bottom was the name
Garth Gautier.

Tears streamed down Miranda's cheeks as
she sat on her bed late that night, reading
and rereading the poems. She saw them differently now, knowing they'd been written by
Garth. Pondering each word, she tried to
imagine what he'd been thinking as he wrote
them, picturing the expression that must
have been on his face as he poured out his
heart to her. At the same time she attempted
to read beyond their obvious meaning, frus-
trated by her inability to discover the reason
for his secretiveness.

Ever since Garth had come into her life,
her feelings for him had grown stronger and
stronger. Finally she had dared to label them
love. She wanted to be close to him, to know
him . . . to understand him. Yet now that she
knew he and her secret admirer were one
and the same, she was more bewildered than
ever. She was being forced to confront the
fact that she really didn't know him at all.

What was this dark side of him? From the
start, when he'd first started leaving her
poems and presents, he'd planned to keep
his distance, to love her from afar without

ever revealing his identity. Yes, he cared for her. She believed that. But even at the beginning, before he'd actually met her, he'd felt the need to hold back.

Perhaps she'd never know why. But there was one thing she did know.

They had shared something magical.

Now it was all coming to an end. While she didn't understand any of it, she did understand that whatever Garth's feelings for her may have been, they weren't strong enough to make him want to fight the demons that were haunting him.

So she would honor his request. She would stay away from him, attempting to control her feelings, to force her head to prevail over her heart. She would try to separate herself from the pain. To go on. Perhaps even to forget.

She would take it on faith that what he'd told her was true: that their love could never be.

"Saint Joan!" barked Tyler Fleming, his irritation only thinly masked. He clapped his hands together. "Where's my Saint Joan?"

Miranda jerked her head up, blinking in confusion. She'd been waiting backstage, sitting on a wooden stool, only vaguely aware of all the bustle going on around her. Usually she loved rehearsals. She found the act of putting together a theatrical production one of the most exhilarating experiences she'd ever had.

She was even intrigued by the more tedious aspects. Waiting while the director discussed the script with other performers. Doing the same scene over and over again, until Tyler Fleming was satisfied. Standing still for a very long time, enduring the hot lights while the technical crew worked out lighting cues that corresponded with the actors' movements on stage.

Tonight, however, she was having trouble concentrating. There was simply too much preying on her mind, too many emotions causing her heart to ache.

Miranda was overcome with a sense of loss. It was difficult for her to believe that less than three weeks ago, she had been happy about how well her life was going. Since then, her entire world had come apart. She'd stood by, watching everything crumbling piece by piece. And the worst part was she'd been completely unable to do a single thing to stop it. Now the final pieces had fallen. Garth

was out of her life. The mysterious admirer
who for weeks had been leaving her poems
and presents was gone as well. Finding out
they were one and the same person had left
her feeling devastated.

This boy Garth, this brooding yet irresistible young man who had so quickly stolen
her heart . . . what was the mystery that en-
shrouded him? she kept wondering.

"I'm not what you think I am," he had told
her. *"There are things about me you don't know."*

What was this terrible secret of his? And
whatever it was, why did it mean that the two
of them had to remain apart . . . two people
who, from the start, had felt such a strong
connection to each other?

Her sorrow from that afternoon after the
memorial service, when Garth had sent her
away, was lodged inside, as agonizing as if it
were a dagger that had been thrust into her
heart. Even as she struggled to banish it, to
concentrate instead on what she loved most
about her life: theater.

And now Tyler Fleming was summoning
her, the annoyance in his tone unmistakable.
She had missed her cue. Miranda hated that
the struggles in her personal life were inter-
fering with her performance. In fact, earlier

that evening, on her way to rehearsal, she had vowed not to let that happen. Yet that was precisely what was going on.

"I'm sorry," she sputtered, jumping off the stool.

Tyler Fleming cast a cold look in her direction. "You must make a point of being aware of what is happening during every second of the performance. Not only you, Miranda. That goes for everyone in the company."

He hesitated, rubbing his eyes tiredly. After glancing at his watch, he said, "All right. Let's take a ten-minute break. We're all beginning to feel the pressure. But I want everyone in scene two back onstage at eight fifteen. Sharp!"

"What's wrong?" Elinor had rushed to Miranda's side after the director's harsh words to Miranda. Distractedly she pushed her straight, light-brown hair back, then stuck the pencil she'd been using to mark her copy of the script behind her ear. "You look like you could use some fresh air. Want to go outside?"

"Thanks, but I'm all right." Miranda had intended to sound strong—matter-of-fact, even. Instead, she suddenly felt her lower lip tremble. Two tears slid down her cheeks.

Immediately Elinor took hold of her arm. "Come with me," she insisted. "I know a place where we can talk."

She led her to a small lounge, furnished with a sagging couch, a few tables, and a vending machine. It was deserted.

"Now tell me." Elinor plopped down on the couch, gesturing for Miranda to join her. "What's going on?"

"It's over." Miranda bit her lip hard, wanting to keep any more tears from falling.

"*What's* over?"

Miranda took a few deep breaths, keeping her gaze fixed on the piping that edged the couch cushions. "Garth. He . . . he broke up with me."

"What happened?" Elinor cried.

"I'm not sure."

"Did it have anything to do with what happened at the dance?"

"I don't know *what* caused it." Miranda leaned forward, burying her face in her hands. There no longer seemed to be any point in trying to hold back the tears. She began to sob, her shoulders shaking and her breaths coming in gasps as she gave in to her anguish.

"Go back to the beginning," Elinor said in

a soothing voice once Miranda's sobs had subsided. "Tell me everything."

Slowly Miranda poured out her story, hesitant at first, then growing more and more animated as she recounted the puzzling events that had led up to Garth's surprising announcement two days before.

"I thought I knew him, Elinor. I thought he and I had something really special between us. I . . . I was in love with him."

"Oh, Miranda!"

"And I know he felt strongly about me. I could see it in his eyes, in the way he looked at me, the way he touched me. . . .

"When I was with Garth, I felt things I'd never felt before. Not only about him, but also about myself. I felt I could accomplish anything I wanted. As if I had the power to be whatever it was I longed to be. I don't know if it makes any sense, but he made me feel really *special.*"

Elinor was nodding. "It makes perfect sense," she said in a quiet voice.

"And now it's over. It could have been something beautiful. Something lasting. The kind of thing that's so rare most people are never lucky enough to experience it. We had that, Elinor. And he took it all away."

Abruptly Elinor stood up. She reached deep inside the front pocket of her jeans, pulling out a crumpled tissue. "Here. Get yourself together. You've got exactly two minutes before you have to get up onstage. And do you know what you're going to do?"

Miranda shook her head, wiping the tears from her face.

"You're going to give Tyler Fleming the performance of a lifetime. I know your heart is breaking, Miranda. But take that emotion, take that energy, and channel it into something you really care about. Something you *love*."

"I—I'm not sure I can."

"I *know* you can. You're strong. That feeling you had when you were Garth is real, Miranda. You *are* capable of doing anything you set your mind to. And that means you can be the actress you always dreamed of being. You can make the character of Joan of Arc come alive."

"I want to, Elinor. I really do."

"Then you will. And as for your heart, just remember: you'll get through this. There's absolutely no doubt in my mind. And having weathered this heartbreak will make you that much stronger."

Miranda sniffled. But she got up off the couch, her posture a little straighter, her head held higher than before.

"You're right. I have to get on with my life."

"That's the spirit."

She put her hand on the doorknob, then looked at Elinor and said, "Thank you."

Elinor looked surprised. "For what? For giving you a tissue? For delivering a pep talk?"

"No." For the first time all evening, Miranda smiled. "For being such a good friend."

CHAPTER
17

Once again the moon was full.

The autumn night was biting, winter's icy fingers already gripping the forest. The sky was black satin, a sharp contrast to the moon, glowing with an eerie brightness.

Tonight, he was not part of the night.

Instead he gazed out the window, narrow panes crisscrossed with the bars of an iron grating.

Purposely he had imprisoned himself. Earlier that evening, he had waited inside Cedar Crest, agonizing over his fate . . . wondering if perhaps he could alter it.

He knew that tonight, the change would come upon him. That the evil presence would wield its power. That once again the beast would be unable to resist.

Yet he was determined to fight the desire to seek out human flesh once again. And so when night began to fall, he had descended into the depths of Cedar Crest, where his only weapon against total blackness was a single hurricane lamp, its pale flame casting long shadows upon the crumbling stone steps and the narrow twisting hallways.

Down in the cellar, among the thick cobwebs and the damp spots where water trickled down through aged cracks, nestled between the now-empty wine cellar and the abandoned storage areas, was a small room. He had been inside only once, puzzling over its purpose.

Now he understood.

It was a prison, of sorts, a cell in which someone—or something—could be locked away, unable to cause harm. The only window was barred. The door was thick wood, so warped that it was wedged firmly into the concrete frame.

The door could be unlocked from the inside, but only with a key hidden in a box by the door, accessible only to the man.

He wasn't sure his plan would work. Yet he had to try. If only this room could contain him while the moon was full! If only it could enforce a control that he himself lacked.

If only this room would keep the werewolf from killing again.

When the moon began to rise, he'd come inside, pushing hard against the door, confident that even the strongest animal would be unable to find a way of getting past it.

Now he waited.

Staring out the window, he watched as the moon continued its climb in the night sky. As it did, the change began. It started with the tingling sensation that electrified his skin. His jaw lengthened, his muscles swelled, the fine golden hairs spurted everywhere. He watched with great curiosity, anxious to see how the beast would react.

Gradually the boy's awareness faded. Once again the beast emerged.

At first it was confused. It blinked hard, unable to comprehend the four gray walls that surrounded it, containing it inside such a small space.

It grew more agitated as it paced, sniffing the walls, searching for a means of escape. It yearned to test its muscles to the limit, to race through the forest. Its senses were as sharp as always, its nostrils flaring as it tried to pick out something familiar, its ears pricked in an attempt at discovering what this place was.

And then, the rage.

Never before had it been contained. Never before had its instinctive drive to roam freely through the forest been restrained.

Never before had its urge to hunt been crushed.

The beast raised its head, on the verge of releasing an agonized howl of defeat.

It was then that it heard the voices.

"Are you sure about this, Corinne?"

"What are you, Devlin, chicken?"

Two boys. They spoke in whispers, their voices edged with fear. The beast froze, its senses even more alert than before.

"Come on, Tommy. Don't back out on us now. You promised, remember?"

A girl, this time.

"Besides, it's just a practical joke. A few firecrackers to let him know he's not welcome in Overlook."

The beast heard their words without understanding them. What it did understand was that there were three of them. Two boys and a girl. Right outside the basement window, coming closer every second.

And it understood that the urge to hunt was overwhelming.

"How are we supposed to get in?" demanded one of the boys. "The front door's locked."

"Haven't you guys learned anything from TV?" The girl's tone was one of exasperation. "We'll break in through the basement. There's probably a door somewhere."

There was a long silence. "I don't know, Corinne," said one of the boys. "That's breaking and entering. Not exactly the same thing as a practical joke."

"You are chicken, aren't you? Well, who needs you? I can do this myself."

"Let's go back, Corinne." The boy sounded even more fearful than before. "Maybe this wasn't such a good idea, after all."

"You go. I can manage. Here, give me that flashlight."

The beast watched through the window, taking care to stay in the shadows. Every muscle was tense. It longed to strike out, to break through the glass.

Yet something inside told it to hold back. To hide in the darkness and wait.

The three of them argued some more, gradually moving out of the beast's range. Once again it began its agitated pacing. It leaped up against the cold stone walls, its head nearly reaching the ceiling. There was no way out.

Anxiously it circled the small space, desperate to escape. And then it froze.

It heard a noise.

It pointed its ears upward. Someone was rattling the rotted wooden door at the end of the corridor.

From the scent, it knew it was the girl.

And then she was inside the house.

"I knew it," she muttered. "An old wreck like this was bound to be easy to get into. Now all I need is a place to light these stupid firecrackers."

The beast stood perfectly still, lurking in the shadowy space next to the door, prepared to pounce. Its nose twitched as the scent of the girl grew stronger.

She was moving closer.

And then, "Are you nuts, Corinne? Let's get out of here!"

One of the boys. He'd come back.

"Look, Paul. I've come this far—"

"If you get caught, you're dead! Come on! Believe me, it's not worth it."

"Oh, all right. You go ahead with Tommy. I'll catch up with you in a minute."

"Do what you want, but Paul and I are outta here."

Her scent was growing weaker. She was moving away. The beast relaxed its stance, lying on the cold stone floor in defeat. It could hear her moving down the corridor. Slowly. Uncertainly.

The footsteps stopped. For a long time, there was silence. It waited, ears pricked, not yet ready to give up.

And then the sound resumed, this time taking a different direction. Suddenly her scent flooded the room. She was pushing against the door.

Instantly the beast was poised. With a great creaking sound, the wooden door moved. In the dim light it saw her silhouette in the doorway.

She paused, blinking. And then, catching sight of the huge form crouching before her, she let out a piercing scream.

She turned and ran, racing through the winding corridor. The beast followed, its massive form an encumbrance in the narrow hallways, its movements slowed down by the slippery floor, the unexpected turns, the unfamiliar space in which even its keen senses could not help it find its way.

And then it was outdoors, the girl rushing toward the woods, ahead of him. Easily it caught up with her. She turned, a look of horror on her face, too frightened even to scream.

A glorious feeling of release washed over the beast. It stood poised for only a moment. And then it pounced, meeting with little resistance as it shoved its victim to the ground.

Miranda sat down on the edge of the back porch and surveyed the work she'd just completed. She'd needed a distraction, a way of taking her mind off the terrible sadness that had of late become too comfortable a companion. And so after spending Sunday afternoon at her father's, she'd come home and begun planting flower bulbs—daffodils and crocuses that, come spring, would burst forth with colorful blossoms.

As she began to work, she wondered if, by the time the flowers bloomed, the raw feelings that gnawed away at her would have been tempered. Perhaps by then she'd be able to think about Garth without feeling as if an important part of herself had been wrenched away.

Just as she'd hoped, throwing herself into something physical did create a sort of peace inside her, a welcome feeling of accomplishment. The sun was completely obscured by clouds, yet she still relished being outdoors. The air was biting, but rather than acting as a deterrent, the rawness energized her. Her cheeks burning with the cold, she called up all her strength, energetically digging in the rich soil and planting new life.

She was about to head inside when she saw Officer Vale crossing the front yard.

"Hello," Miranda greeted her tentatively, remembering the unhappy circumstances of their last meeting.

When Miranda caught sight of the somber expression on Officer Vale's face, a feeling of dread crept over her.

"What is it?" she demanded, her voice hoarse.

"Miranda, can we go inside and sit down?"

Miranda remained frozen to the spot. "Have you found out who killed Andy?"

"I really think we should sit down—"

"Tell me." Her voice was so strained even she barely recognized it.

Officer Vale took a deep breath. "There's been another attack."

"Who?"

"Corinne Davis."

Everything stopped. And then a single

mournful syllable escaped Miranda's lips.

"*No!*"

It was all Miranda could do to drag herself into school Monday morning. She was exhausted, having been unable to sleep at all the night before. Pedaling toward the school building, moving in slow motion, she wondered how she would ever get through the day.

At least Corinne was still alive. Officer Vale had said she was in the county hospital, badly hurt but in stable condition. She would be all right—at least physically.

It was her psyche the doctors were concerned about. The trauma she'd suffered had left her in a state of delirium, unable to remember anything about her attack, barely able to speak at all.

As she made her way across the schoolyard, toward the door, Miranda braced herself. Today, she knew, would be reserved for class discussions about what had happened. First Andy. Now Corinne. Two incidents in a little less than a month, both involving seniors at Overlook High. Two grotesque attacks, twenty-nine days apart.

One was someone she barely knew, the

other a close friend for a decade. One had died and one had been lost to her with bad feelings still lingering between them. Lurking right beneath the surface of Miranda's sorrow was the nagging feeling that somehow, in a way she couldn't possibly explain, she'd had something to do with it.

She was deep in thought as she turned the corner on her way to her locker and nearly collided with Selina, her eyes ringed with red. Standing next to her was Amy Patterson.

"Well, well, well. Look who's here." The coldness in Selina's voice was a surprising contrast to her look of grief. "So how does it feel, knowing your archrival is out of the picture?"

"Archrival? What are you talking about?"

"Ironic, isn't it? Even if Corinne had gotten the part, she wouldn't have been able to go ahead with it. The role of Saint Joan would have been yours regardless. Funny how things work out."

"I'm really not interested in continuing this conversation," Miranda insisted. "Now, if you'll just let me pass—"

"Maybe you've heard all you want to hear, but I haven't finished saying all I want to say." Selina's eyes narrowed into slits. "Corinne is lying in a hospital right now, Miranda. She was almost killed! And what kind of friend were you to her? It would have been so easy for you to make sure she got the lead in that play. It would've meant so much to her!"

"Please, Selina. I can't do this right now. If you'll just excuse me—"

The two girls didn't budge.

"Have you noticed, Amy," Selina said, her large green eyes fixed on Miranda, "that there's a definite connection between the two kids who were attacked?"

The blond girl's eyes widened. "What do you mean?"

"They were both enemies of Miranda's."

Miranda had had it. "Corinne and I weren't enemies! Maybe we were going through a rough period, but you know as well as I do that she and I had been friends practically forever. And I hardly even knew Andy!"

Amy ignored what she'd said. "You're right, Selina. What an odd coincidence."

Selina folded her arms across her chest. "Maybe she and that boyfriend of hers were out for revenge."

"What are you talking about?" Fury was rising inside Miranda. "How could you even think such a thing?"

"It's not as if I'm the only one," Selina countered.

Amy nodded. "Rumors are flying."

Miranda was on the verge of tears. "Please let me go. All I want right now is to be alone!"

She pushed her way through the crowd of students in the corridor, wishing it were all a dream. She wished she'd never tried out for the play. She wished that she and Corinne were still friends. For the hundredth time in the past few weeks, she wished everything could simply go back to the way it used to be.

Immediately after school, Miranda headed for the Overlook library. She needed to see Garth. She couldn't put it off any longer. For a full month she had respected his wishes, keeping away from him. She had even ridden into Norton whenever she'd needed books. Yet she'd thought about him constantly, feeling a sense of loss so great it was almost a physical pain.

Her stomach tightened as she stood in the middle of the library, looking for him. He wasn't there.

She headed toward the front desk. "Excuse me, Ms. Wallace," she said, "I'm looking for Garth Gautier. Has he been in lately?"

"Garth? Oh, yes. The studious boy." The woman peered at Miranda through her glasses. "He hasn't been around here for ages. A few weeks, at least."

Miranda was already racing out of the building. Her adrenaline was pumping as she jumped on her bike and headed out toward Winding Way.

I have to find him, she was thinking. Please, *please* make him be there!

Arriving at Cedar Crest, the tires of her bicycle bumping over the rough dirt road, she was struck once again by the stillness of the place. The house, too, seemed even more silent and ominous than last time. Today the windows, so many eyes staring blankly ahead, seemed to look right through her, mocking her with their indifference. Shadows loomed everywhere, as if hiding something that didn't want its presence known. The house looked abandoned, so desolate it was, as if this were the place in which loneliness itself dwelled.

Miranda's heart pounded as she grabbed hold of the brass knocker and banged on the front door. She was afraid of seeing him again—afraid he would send her away. Yet even that risk was not too much to take. She knew, deep inside, that she simply had to try.

She stood for a long time, listening to the clanging of the brass knocker echoing through the house's empty rooms.

He was gone.

This was what she'd feared most. Learning that there was not even the remotest chance of seeing him again. That never again would she be able to look at him, speak with him . . . know he was near.

Something had convinced him he had no choice but to leave. She thought of the terrible rumors circulating around school, then shook her head as if to banish them from her mind. But there was something, perhaps the terrible secret he'd persisted in keeping from her . . .

Yet instinctively she knew that it was her doing. It was his love for her that, for reasons she would never understand, drove him away.

Sinking down onto the crumbling stone steps of Cedar Crest, blanketed by the silence, Miranda wept. Her love for Garth was pure and undemanding, as selfless as it was unrelenting. Yet in the end, it was that love that had driven him away.

"Miranda?"

Miranda was lying on the bed, furiously scrawling in her diary, pouring her feelings out onto its blank pages. She'd been feeling so alone . . . yet she'd desperately wanted someone to confide in. She'd *needed* someone to confide in. Someone who would listen, someone who wouldn't pass judgment. The only place she knew she could turn to was her diary.

The sound of a human voice came as a surprise. Glancing up, she saw that her mother was standing in the doorway. Mrs. Campbell's expression was serious. And when she'd spoken her daughter's name, her voice had been filled with concern.

"Yes, Mom?" Miranda closed her journal, keeping her pen inside to mark her place.

"If you're not busy, I thought you and I might talk."

"All right."

Her mother edged over to the bed and sat down. "Working on your homework?"

"No. I was just writing in my diary."

Mrs. Campbell smiled. "I kept a diary when I was a teenager, too. I still have it. It's funny; I always thought that once I grew up, I'd go back and pore over every word. But even though I've hung on to it, I've never actually reread what I wrote."

"Why not?"

Pensive, she said, "I'm not sure. Maybe it's because that was such a special time in my life that I feel there's something sacred about the confidences I wrote down then. I was so emotional when I was that age. The tiniest, most insignificant things seemed to take on such earth-shattering proportions. Everything mattered to the person I was back then."

With a little shrug, she added, "Somehow, looking back into that period of my life, judging it from where I am now, seems unfair. Disrespectful, in a way."

"What were you like when you were a teenager, Mom?"

Mrs. Campbell reached over and pushed a strand of hair out of her daughter's eyes. "I was a lot like you, sweetie. I felt things very deeply, too." Mrs. Campbell paused before adding, "Honey, I'm worried about you."

"I'm all right." Miranda's words sounded false, even to her. "It's just that this is turning out to be kind of a complicated time for me."

"And your father and me splitting up isn't doing anything to help, is it?"

"I know it's not your fault, Mom. It's not

Daddy's either. But that—combined with everything else that's been going on—is making me feel as if my life has been turned upside down."

"I know the feeling." Mrs. Campbell smiled sadly.

Miranda bit her lip. She didn't want to add to the pressures she knew her mother was already under, but it felt so good to be talking to her. She realized it had been a long time since she'd really confided in her mother. Probably *too* long.

"Mom," she said tentatively, "is Daddy the only man you were ever in love with?"

"Oh, no." A flush rose on Mrs. Campbell's cheeks. "When I was just about your age—I was sixteen—I fell in love with a boy at school."

"Was he in love with you, too?"

"Yes. We were crazy about each other. It was such a wonderful feeling. It would have been even more wonderful, though, if there hadn't been one major problem."

"What was that?"

"He and I were very different. I was a straight-A student, very conscientious and eager to please, very concerned with doing what my parents wanted me to do. And this boy . . . well, he was a bit of a rebel."

"How romantic!" Miranda exclaimed, then laughed. She could hardly believe this was her mother talking.

"Yes, I suppose it does sound romantic. But at the time, it was very painful. You see, I knew my parents would never approve. My friends, either. I was so torn. I had to make a decision."

"What did you choose?"

Miranda's mother cast her a look of regret. "I wasn't strong enough to fight for him."

She hesistated for a long time before adding, "For years I wondered how things would have turned out if I'd had the courage to follow through on my feelings. If I'd recognized that what the two of us had was really special . . . and insisted on seeing it through. I dated other men as I got older, but the feelings I had for them never came close to what I'd felt for that boy. Then I met your father. I fell head over heels in love with him. It wasn't long before I decided he was the man I wanted to spend the rest of my life with."

Mrs. Campbell lowered her eyes. Miranda wasn't certain, but she thought they had grown shiny with tears.

"Do you know what happened to that boy?"

"No. We lost touch." Miranda's mother waved her hand in the air. "You know how it is. People grow up, they move on. . . ."

She turned to face Miranda. "Honey, I know this isn't really any of my business. But I couldn't help noticing how upset you've been. And I keep wondering if it has something to do with Garth."

After thinking for a few moments, Miranda nodded. "He—we broke up."

"Oh, Miranda! I'm so sorry! I could see you really cared about him." She took hold of Miranda's hand and said, "Sometimes it's very difficult being a mother. When you were a little girl, I tried to protect you as much as I could. And I managed to do that, up to a point. I kept you away from things that could cut you or scratch you, I watched to make sure you didn't wander out of the yard, I scooped you up into my arms every time we saw a big dog or even a scary-looking cat when we were out walking.

"But now that you're older, I realize there are many things I can't protect you from. All I can say is that I know how you're feeling. And that no matter what happens out in the world, you'll always be able to count on one thing. And that's that I love you."

Miranda could feel the tears streaming down her face. Tears of sorrow, but also tears of relief, of gratitude . . . of love. She threw her arms around her mother, clinging to her in the same way she had when she was a little girl.

She knew her mother was right. She couldn't protect her daughter from heartache. Still, knowing that she had felt similar feelings—was feeling them now, in fact—and was nevertheless managing to carry on, did make Miranda feel better. She felt so close to her. At the same time, she realized her relationship with her mother was changing.

It was true Miranda was no longer a little girl, someone to be protected. She was beginning to make her own way in the world. And that was a long and arduous process, one that was bound to include failures as well as triumphs. Self-doubts as well as growing confidence. Fear as well as optimism.

Heartache as well as love.

It was all part of growing up into an adult, she now understood; part of making the transition from being a little girl to being a woman.

CHAPTER
18

Miranda stood in front of the dressing-room mirror, scrutinizing her reflection. It was difficult to believe that after two long months of rehearsals, it was finally opening night. For the past month, she'd thrown herself into the play, desperate for a way to cope with the horrific events of a few weeks earlier: the attack on Corinne, the state of shock she'd slipped into as a result, Garth's abrupt disappearance.

Now the period of preparation, of anticipation, was over. In less than fifteen minutes she'd be standing onstage, delivering her opening lines—this time to a packed auditorium. She was surprised she wasn't more nervous. Rather than the butterflies she'd expected, she instead experienced a kind of fascination as she studied the girl in the mirror.

What amazed her most was that it wasn't Miranda Campbell who stared back at her. It was Joan, the Maid of Orléans.

The dress that Ann Stevens had created was breathtaking. The deep-red velvet fabric highlighted her rosy skin tones. It was expertly cut so that the bodice was clingy, the low neckline dramatic, the skirt flowing, its soft folds falling gently to the floor.

The stage makeup she'd recently learned to apply emphasized her features: her eyelashes were even thicker, the blush of her cheeks even more pronounced, her dark red lips even fuller. For the play's opening, her hair was left wild and free, its soft waves forming a sort of halo about her face and shoulders. She looked every inch the country girl: free-spirited, courageous, still unsuspecting of the trials that lay ahead.

Miranda's dreamy mood was broken by a sharp knock at the door.

"Ten minutes to curtain, Miranda," Elinor called.

"Thank you."

It was then that she was struck by the momentousness of what she was about to do.

The entire production rested on her shoulders. Yes, she had the support of the cast and crew members, and no one could deny that this was a group effort. But just as in the case of the real Saint Joan, she was their leader.

Once she ventured out of the dressing room, Miranda witnessed the members of the backstage crew rushing around frantically amidst the cables and scenery and racks of costumes. A technician was reviewing lighting cues, and the makeup artist fussed with the squire's powdered wig. She was pleased when Elinor glanced up from the clipboard she and the stage manager were studying to smile, meanwhile mouthing, "Break a leg!"

She felt someone tap her on the shoulder. Turning, she saw Ann Stevens studying her, a smile of approval on her face.

"Miranda Campbell," the costume director said, "you are a vision."

Laughing, she retorted, "I'm supposed to be the one *having* the visions, remember?"

Ann continued to survey the dress, meanwhile tugging at the skirt, adjusting the neckline. "I must say, I've really outdone myself. Of course, I had quite a bit of inspiration."

Miranda reached over and gave the woman's hand a squeeze.

"Come. I have something to show you."
Ann led her closer to the stage, then reached
over and pulled back the curtain. "Stand here
and you can see the audience. Looks like
we've got a full house tonight."

Peering out, Miranda saw quite a few faces
she recognized: friends, neighbors, students
from her school. As she surveyed the crowd,
however, she was struck with the realization
that there was one person in particular she
was searching for. She yearned to see a head
full of thick golden curls illuminated by the
houselights.

As she'd expected, he wasn't there.

She didn't have long to dwell on her disappointment. The houselights were already
growing dim. The audience settled down, its
rustling fading to a silence heavy with expectation. Miranda's heart was pounding—with
nervousness, with excitement, with a euphoria she knew would carry her through the
next two hours.

She moved toward the stage to wait for
her entrance cue. Already Miranda Campbell
was fading into the background; a spirited
seventeen-year-old who saved an entire country came forth to take her place.

*   *   *

He lurked in the shadows in the back of the theater, waiting for the houselights to dim, wanting to be sure Miranda didn't spot him. He had tried to stay away. He wanted to protect her, not only from what he'd done, but also from what he was. Twice since he'd come to Overlook he'd lost control, finding himself unable to fight the evil forces that consumed him. It was after that second attack that he'd fled, no longer able to deny the fact that he was completely powerless.

For three days he hid in the woods. Wanting to see no one. Wanting no one to see him.

Feeling as if he'd lost whatever right he'd had to be a part of the human race.

Still, he'd been unable to escape the pain. In a small grocery store along the coast, the newspaper headlines taunted him: "Coastal Attacker Strikes Again!" And in smaller letters: "Police Puzzled: Man or Beast?"

Finally he'd gone back to Portland. He expected the crowded streets and sidewalks to offer him the relief of anonymity. Yet even there, he'd been on guard. Afraid to make eye contact. Afraid to be recognized.

Afraid. Always afraid.

Finally he'd retreated to a rooming house

on the outskirts of the city. The paint on the walls was peeling, the bed frame made of smooth metal that was cold to the touch. Through an open window, jammed so that it wouldn't close, a sordid world of neon and noise assaulted him night and day.

None of it mattered. He felt safe in that run-down area, secure in the certainty he was unlikely to run into anyone he knew.

He spent long exhausting days trying to push the thoughts away, and even longer sleepless nights replaying scenes over and over again in his mind.

In the end, he'd been unable to stay away.

He'd snuck back in the night, growing more and more anxious to see Cedar Crest once again. As he traveled through town on foot, he saw the posters, taped to the windows of the shops, nailed to the telephone poles. He paused to read them in the pale light of a waxing moon.

"The Pacific Players Present *Saint Joan*," the bold letters read.

And right underneath, her name.

The longing to see her again, just once more, was excruciating. As he stood in front of the Overlook Grocery, his eyes devouring the words "Miranda Campbell," his heart nearly stopped beating.

Yes, he hungered to see her. It was a craving, as strong as any he'd ever known. Yet he knew he had no choice but to fight the temptation.

Especially because, on opening night, there would be a full moon.

In the end, he'd been powerless to resist. The day of the play, as he agonized over whether or not to stay away, he knew his heart would prevail. Anxiously he watched the clock, cursing the achingly slow movement of its hands, yearning to see her again, the desire so great it had become a need.

Just this once. And then, he promised himself, never again.

Peering inside the open doors of the Playhouse, he saw the lights dim. Realizing that it was now only a question of minutes before he would be in the same room with her, he found it difficult to catch his breath.

Stealthily he slipped inside. The auditorium was packed, making it easy for him to lose himself in the crowd. His eyes were fixed on the stage as he found a seat in the back row.

And then, after all the waiting, after all the

torment, his dream was realized. There she was, onstage.

Miranda.

How beautiful she was! How graceful, how confident. Standing up on the stage, so capable, so sure of herself—he saw that the strength he had always sensed inside this fragile-looking girl was now on the surface, for everyone to see.

Seeing her at such a distance, in the midst of a crowd, did nothing to quell his passion. As he watched, the pain in his heart grew stronger, his longing deepened.

As his eyes remained fixed upon her, however, something ominous descended upon him.

It was suffocating him, this evil presence.

He also sensed that it was laughing at him.

It knows, he thought. *It knows what I am feeling . . . and it knows what is going to happen.*

Whatever it was, it was going to be deadly.

He knew then it had been a mistake to come back.

This time, when his skin began to tingle, along with the familiar feelings of expectation he also experienced fear. It was too late to get back to Cedar Crest, too late to lock himself in the prison room again. And he had a sense that once again he would be unable to resist the temptation of human flesh.

He sat in the auditorium, feeling his connection with all that was around him weakening. The stage suddenly seemed far away, the faces around him smeared into blurs, the walls swirled around him as if he were on a merry-go-round. The urge to flee was coming upon him, causing the muscles in his arms and legs to twitch expectantly.

The bright lights were just beginning to invade his field of vision when something caught his eye. Up on stage, the final scene of the play was underway.

He watched in horror as Miranda—his Miranda—was dragged to a wooden stake. Her hands were tied behind her back with a length of ragged rope. Pieces of wood were piled at her feet.

Through it all, her expression was one of resignation. Of trust. Of peace.

He had seen that expression before.

At the memory of the horrible vision that had come to him at Cedar Crest, his heart began to pound. He watched the stage, spellbound, as a puff of smoke billowed upward. Hideous curls, thick and black, surrounded her. The crowd onstage was chanting. Loud, angry cries rose from their midst.

He could hear the fear in their voices.

Even more, he could feel her fear.

It was as if it were his own.

Once he'd been made to pay for what he was.

A plea suddenly registered in his brain: Please, please, don't let this be my destiny.

Save me.

And then the image of Miranda surrounded by flames faded. Instead, he was swept away by the change. His skin felt as if it were burning up, his senses so acute he shut his eyes against the light, covered his ears against the noise. A terrible feeling of being closed in rushed over him.

He had to get out. He needed to be in the forest.

Outside, the air was fresh and inviting. He headed into the woods, barely having time to pull off his clothes before he felt himself evolving completely into the beast. Sprinting over the forest floor, he looked down. Already there were fine golden hairs all over his body. He flexed his muscles, delighting in their animal strength.

Yet even as he raced through the woods,

basking in the feeling of freedom, a sense of dread overshadowed his delight. He knew that this time, it was different. This time, the change had come on faster.

The evil force was growing more powerful.

No! a voice deep inside cried, frightened by how quickly he was being swept away.

And then that voice faded. It continued to echo through his brain, but the meaning of what it was saying became undecipherable.

Once again, the boy was gone.

The beast was anxious to hunt.

The terrible hunger rose up inside it. It was the new hunger, the one that could not be satisfied by rabbits and squirrels.

It sensed, somewhere deep inside, that tonight its desire would know no bounds.

It stood in the forest, its golden fur glinting in the bright light of the full moon, gracefully poised as it sniffed the air. It hesitated for only a moment. Then it bounded through the forest, determined to fulfill its most basic need, to give in to an instinct that could not go unheeded.

CHAPTER
19

"Brava! Brava!"

The words of praise echoed through the auditorium as Miranda stood alone in center stage, taking her third curtain call. In her arms she cradled a bouquet of red roses, a gift from the rest of the cast, which was an odd contrast to the suit of armor she was wearing. She felt ecstatic. The audience's enthusiasm over her performance was exhilarating, catapulting her to great heights, as if somehow she had risen to become one with the moon and the stars.

Finally the crowd let her go. She hurried backstage, still overwhelmed by their reception. She'd expected to sneak off to the solitude of her dressing room. Instead, she discovered that the entire cast and crew were gathered in the wings, waiting to congratulate her.

"You were fantastic!" Ann Stevens cried, throwing her arms around her.

"Great job, Saint Joan." The man who'd played the squire grinned. "In fact, when it was time for you to be burned at the stake, I was tempted to say, 'Aw, let her go.' "

Miranda laughed. "You were pretty great yourself."

She was flattered by how complimentary everyone was being. Yet even as the troupe's accolades warmed her heart, she was struck by the fact that someone was missing. She would have loved to have shared this moment with Garth.

Her sadness passed when she noticed two familiar faces in the crowd: her mother and her father, both of them wearing broad smiles.

"Oh, Miranda. You were magnificent!" Her mother gave her a big hug.

Her father was beaming. "We're so proud of you, honey."

"Thank you." Smiling broadly, Miranda picked one of the roses out of her bouquet and handed it to her mother. Then she gave one to her father.

"There," she announced. "Now everyone will know we're a family."

"Attention! May I please have everyone's attention?" All of a sudden Taylor Fleming was standing among them, clapping his hands sharply. An expectant silence fell immediately.

"I'd like to congratulate each and every one of you for the first-rate performance you put on tonight. Without exception, you all did admirably. My cast, my crew, you deserve my applause—and my gratitude." The director's dark eyes were shining.

"I'd like everyone to assemble onstage in five minutes for photographs. There are people here tonight from some of the local newspapers—as well as one or two from Portland—who are anxious to make you all even more famous than you already are."

The group laughed. Miranda's mother leaned over and gave her shoulder a squeeze, saying softly, "Guess we'll be going. I'll see you at home."

Before Miranda had a chance to tell her parents how pleased she was to see them both here tonight, Tyler Fleming was at her side.

"Miranda," he said, smiling warmly, "you

were wonderful tonight. It's a big responsibility, taking on the lead role—especially in a drama that's as ambitious as this one. But you did it—and you handled it like a professional. You should be very pleased."

"Thank you." She could feel her cheeks burning. The praise from the play's director meant more to her than anyone else's.

"For the cast photos," he went on, "why don't you change into your costume from the first scene? I'm sure you'd much rather be immortalized in velvet than in chain metal."

Miranda started to hurry off to the dressing room. But then she turned back.

"Mr. Fleming?"

"Yes, Miranda?"

"Thank you for giving me this opportunity. Being in this play has meant a lot to me. And, well, I just want you to know how much I appreciate the faith you've had in me."

He hesitated for a few seconds. "The first time I saw you," he finally said, "I just knew you were my Saint Joan. I sensed that you possessed some of that same spirit, that same courage."

Miranda was still on cloud nine as she headed toward the side door of the Play-

house. The praise of the cast members and
the director, the accolades of so many members of the audience who'd made a point of
coming backstage, the photography session
for the newspapers . . . It had been exhilarating. She had savored every moment.

Even now, she was reluctant to end it.
She'd opted to wear her costume home,
wanting to luxuriate in the feeling of being
swathed in rich, red velvet just a little bit
longer. Its thick folds swirled about her feet,
making her feel every bit the romantic heroine. She still held her bouquet, its red blossoms bursting with sweet fragrance.

As she leaned against the wooden door, a
powerful gust of wind fought her, its piercing
coldness blasting through the doorway. It
took all Miranda's strength to push it open.
As she did, the iciness made her shiver.
Wrapping her arms around herself protec-
tively, she stepped out into the night.

The frigid November sky was a black ex-
panse, unlit by stars. The only light came
from the full moon. The glowing circle was
distant and unfriendly. Miranda walked
quickly, remembering the warnings about
walking alone at night, particularly near the
forest. Still, the yearning to be outdoors, to

exult in the evening's success where she felt happy and free, was too great to ignore.

Even so, when she heard someone call to her, she started.

"Miranda?"

"Elinor!" she said, relieved.

"Wasn't it fantastic?" Elinor was beaming as she ran to catch up with her. "The audience was really with us. Couldn't you feel it? And you were terrific, Miranda."

"Thanks. And you're right; it was great. By the way, thanks for your help. One thing I've learned from all this is how important the people who work backstage are."

"No problem! Want to come over? It's late, but I know I won't be able to sleep tonight."

"Sounds great."

As the two girls began walking, the lights of the theater growing distant and the darkness of the frigid night enveloping them, they were silent. It was Elinor who finally spoke, her tone hesitant.

"Miranda, I—I don't know if I should tell you this—"

"What?"

Elinor took a deep breath. Even in the pale light of the moon Miranda could see how distraught she was. "I'm almost positive I saw Garth sitting in back of the auditorium."

Miranda grabbed hold of her arm. "Garth?" she breathed, hardly daring to say his name. "Are you sure?"

"If it isn't our very own Saint Joan," a harsh voice suddenly interrupted.

The two girls turned. Standing there was Selina, hands on hips. Amy was right behind her, along with Selina's boyfriend, Tommy Devlin.

"So, Miranda," Selina said coldly. "How did it feel, being in the spotlight tonight?"

"It was . . . great." Miranda glanced at Elinor, but her friend's expression reflected the same confusion she was feeling.

"Did you think about Corinne at all? About how she's lying in bed at home, still bandaged up, still unable to remember a thing about what happened that night—"

Miranda closed her eyes. "Selina, please don't do this."

Selina took a step forward, her eyes flashing. "The part of Joan of Arc *should* have gone to Corinne. *She* should have been the one wearing that dress."

Tommy Devlin held up his hands. "Look, it's too late to change any of this. What's the point, Selina?"

"He's right," said Elinor. "It's not as if there was anything anyone could have done."

Tommy swallowed hard. "Maybe if Paul and I had stayed with her, maybe if all three of us had made the trip home through the woods together . . ." His voice trailed off.

"Have you thought about how it must have been for her, Miranda?" Selina moved closer to Miranda, putting her face right up next to hers. "Do you think about her alone in the woods, in the dark, suddenly hearing somebody rush out at her? Or maybe she didn't hear him. Maybe she didn't even know until it was too late to run, until he'd grabbed her and pulled her to the ground—"

"Stop!" Miranda clamped her hands over her ears. "Please, stop!"

"Come on, Miranda. Let's get out of here." Elinor grabbed her arm and began dragging her away. "We don't have to listen to this."

Miranda was in tears as she followed Elinor, nearly tripping over the hem of her long dress. What had only minutes before been one of the finest nights of her life was quickly turning into one of the most painful.

As she hurried down the path behind Elinor, she suddenly felt compelled to glance up at the full moon. As she did, she found herself hoping the worst was over.

What had before seemed to her such a beautiful night now seemed ominous.

"What hurts most," she finally said, her voice strained, "is that Selina and Corinne and I were all best friends. We used to be so close. And then—"

She couldn't go on. It was a relief when a car pulled up beside them and Ann Stevens's smiling face peeked out from an open window.

"Still flying high?" she asked.

Biting her lip, Miranda nodded.

"Me, too. It makes me so proud to see you in that costume."

"It's an incredible dress," Elinor said.

"Can I offer you girls a ride home?" Ann asked.

"Thanks," said Miranda. "But it's such a nice night, I think we'd rather walk."

Ann frowned. "Are you sure you'll be all right out here alone?"

"We'll be fine," Elinor assured her. "But thank you, anyway." She waved as the car took off.

The girls' route home led them off the

main road, along the edge of the forest. Clumps of bushes lined the path, draped in shadow, their odd shapes ominous. As they walked, Miranda tried to keep the conversation going, without much luck. She was making small talk about the play when she suddenly felt Elinor grab her arm.

"Wait. Did you hear something?"

"It was probably just the wind," Miranda insisted. Still, she glanced nervously over her shoulder. There was nothing, only shadows shifting like the glass panes of a kaleidoscope. The air was strangely still.

The girls continued on, this time in silence. A loud cracking sound caused them both to stop in their tracks.

"I heard that." This time Miranda grabbed hold of Elinor. Her voice was hoarse, betraying her fear.

"Maybe it was an animal." Elinor didn't sound convincing. "A raccoon or . . . or a deer."

Miranda glanced at her nervously. "You don't think Amy and Selina followed us, do you?"

"I doubt it." Elinor swallowed hard. "Maybe we should have taken Ann up on her offer."

"It's not that much farther to your house.

I'm sure we'll be fine." Miranda's voice was pinched.

And then one of the dark shadows alongside the path shifted and a black shape rose up from behind the bushes.

Leaping toward them was a wolf.

Miranda froze. She was vaguely aware that beside her Elinor was screaming.

It was the largest wolf Miranda had ever seen. Its chest was massive, moving with such speed that it was only seconds before it was close enough for her to see its powerful muscles. Gigantic paws lunged toward her, bringing the beast closer and closer. Its sharp teeth were bared, gleaming white in the light of the moon.

Yet even in her terror, Miranda was struck by the fact that its tremendous size and power were only part of what made it unlike any such animal she had ever seen.

Its fur was not the dark gray or black of other wolves. It was golden.

Still, there was no time to think. The animal was heading straight for Elinor.

"Oh, my God!" Elinor yelled, recoiling. She held her arms up, as if somehow she could find the strength to fight off the beast. For a split second, there was a horrible feeling of inevitability. And then, as if through a miracle, a surge of strength rose up inside Miranda.

Before she'd even had a chance to think about what she was doing, she leaped in front of Elinor. She acted on impulse, never stopping to think that she, too, would be powerless in the face of such a muscular animal. She knew only that she had to protect her friend.

The beast was about to come in for the kill when in the bright light of the full moon, Miranda saw its eyes.

They were blue.

In an instant, she understood.

The beast froze, its eyes locked on hers. Every muscle in Miranda's body tensed. She closed her eyes, a low moan escaping her lips. In a sudden burst—so strong, so powerful, that it was completely out of her control— Miranda felt her own strength rushing into him.

The strength to resist. The strength to fight.

The strength to overcome whatever evil force it was that motivated him to destroy.

When she opened her eyes, gasping for breath, she saw that the golden beast had turned away. He was fleeing, returning to the forest in defeat.

She felt his shame. His pain was her pain.

And then a feeling of terrible desperation washed over her. Miranda threw back her head, closing her eyes against the light of the moon, now blindingly bright. A single syllable escaped her lips, a plaintive cry, a plea.

"*Garth!*"

In that simple word was embodied all the love, all the hope, all the life she had ever known.

CHAPTER
20

The torment was so great he feared it would consume him.

He roamed the forest, his heart heavy with remorse and shame. His hunger had been forgotten. The gnawing emptiness in his stomach was nothing compared to the intense loneliness that ate away at him.

Finally she understood. He had seen it in her eyes. The shock. The horror. Above all, the pain he had caused her.

The thing he had feared most had finally come to pass.

She now knew him for what he really was.

Throwing back his head, he let out a mournful howl. Yes, he was still a beast, a werewolf, a tortured soul destined to undergo shapeshifting every twenty-nine days.

But this time, the line between the man and the beast was thinly drawn.

This time, his body was that of an animal . . . but his mind was that of a human.

She had done this. Her power, her strength, had weakened the pull of whatever source of evil was responsible. She had instilled in him a sense of control unlike any he had ever before experienced under the full moon.

Miranda had kept him from killing.

Her love for him had been so strong that when it came face to face with the evil power, love had triumphed.

Still, he knew that he did not deserve that love. How could he, when two times he had killed? And the last—he could still feel the fear of that girl who had fallen beneath his terrible claws. How could he, when his legacy was to change into a monstrous beast every time the moon was full?

How could he deserve her love, when he lacked the strength to combat the dark forces that preyed upon him?

And so he wandered through the woods, keeping himself hidden. Loathing what he was. Wishing it could be different.

Knowing it never could.

And then, as if being led by some mysterious force, he found himself at the edge of a lake. He was far inland, he knew, farther than he usually traveled during his nighttime forays.

The lake was beautiful, stretching out before him like a sheet of glass. The bright light of the full moon glinted off the tiny ripples in its surface.

He sensed the water was deep.

He understood then why he had been brought to this spot. The evil force had led him here, to his destiny.

He stood at the edge of the lake, imagining how it would feel. Plunging into the icy water. Allowing it to surround him, to overpower him, to suck him down into its depths. Relinquishing control.

For a moment he was certain it was the only path to follow. He yearned to let go, to give it up. To end the torment.

To admit defeat.

And yet, despite the lure of abandoning the fight, there was some other force acting on him as well. The full moon was still in the sky—gazing down at him, as always seeming to mock him—yet the dark blue horizon was already growing paler. The morning mist, as

thick and white as a veil, was settling in over
the forest, working its way into the deep shadows, covering the darkness like the first snow-
fall.

Soon the night would end. He was already
changing, shifting back to a man. He could
feel his muscles losing some of their strength.
The golden hairs covering his limbs were
growing sparse. His jaw was getting smaller,
his features beginning the metamorphosis
from those of an animal to those of a human.

And then suddenly he saw something
move. He turned, suddenly tense. There had
been a movement from deep inside the forest.

He was not alone.

He peered through the mist, curious
about who—or what—was seeking him out.
He braced himself, expecting to feel the presence of evil.

Instead it was as if a beam of light were
penetrating the darkness that had befallen
him.

She emerged through the white swirls of
fog. Her long dark hair, wild and free, framed
the soft, gentle features of her face. Her
expression was one of total serenity. All-
knowing. Forgiving. Gracefully she walked

across the forest floor, holding up the hem of her red velvet gown to keep it from getting caught on the brambles.

He watched, spellbound. She looked like a vision.

But she wasn't a vision. She was real.

His Miranda was coming to him.

His first instinct was to flee. To hide from her in shame.

But there was determination in her step as she made her way toward him, a certainty that what she was doing was the right thing.

From her, he garnered strength. He stood before her, half man, half beast. Prepared, for the very first time, to show her what he was. To risk her rejection. Her repulsion. Her scorn.

The moon's glow was fading as the darkness of the night recoiled in deference to the approaching dawn. Yet even in the pale light, as he took a step toward her, he could see the love shining in her dark eyes.

Miranda walked as if she were in a daze, her eyes wide and unseeing, her movements languorous. As she emerged from the depths of the forest, making her way toward the lake in an almost dreamlike state, she didn't know what to expect. Still, there was nothing that could have prepared her for the half man, half beast she found standing at the edge of the lake.

Even so, she saw only Garth, her Garth. And rather than feeling repelled, she felt only love.

Seeing him before, looking into his eyes, she had finally known what he had tried so hard to keep her from knowing. Suddenly she understood all the things that before had made no sense. Garth, her love, was cursed. He was destined to spend his life as a man . . . and an animal. Some terrible force—something outside him, something evil—controlled his destiny. And he was powerless in its grasp.

Having finally reached that understanding made her love for him even stronger.

"You came," he said, his voice hoarse.

"Yes," she said simply.

As she studied him, his expression was tense and uncertain. His face was the same—his blue eyes, his strong features—yet fine golden hairs clung to his cheeks. While his hair was still the same shade of gold, its texture was that of a wolf's fur, thick and smooth and gleaming.

"You want to be with me, Miranda? Even now when you finally understand—?"

She held a finger up to his lips, then reached for his hand. It was oddly heavy, still covered with fur. She brought it up to her lips and gently kissed it. Looking into his eyes, she said, "I love you."

She felt him stiffen. "How could you possibly love me, now that you know what I really am?"

"Don't you see?" she cried. "It's a relief, finally being able to understand."

She squeezed his hand. "It's true that I know now what you are, Garth. But it doesn't matter. I can't deny what's in my heart. You and I belong together."

"Oh, Miranda, you make me feel so strong," Garth said. He lay his hand against her cheek. "Before, when I was out of control, I could feel your strength. It was as if your love and your belief in me surged into my very soul. It was the first time I've ever felt I could fight."

"I felt it, too," said Miranda. "And I understood, in that moment, as I understand now, that our love is your only hope."

"Then you'll stay with me? Please, Miranda. Tell me you'll stay. Say you'll help me!"

She knelt down and reached for him, encircling his neck and drawing him close to her. His breath was warm against her chest, his cheek softer even than the velvet of her gown.

In the pink and yellow light of the dawn she could see their reflection in the lake's glassy surface. The two of them, clinging to each other. Experiencing a love so deep and so pure that no obstacle—not even this— could stand in its way. Knowing that a fierce struggle lay ahead, yet believing with all their might that in the end they would prevail.

"Of course I'll stay," Miranda said, her voice soft, yet filled with resolve. "Together you and I can overcome this, Garth. Together, we can overcome anything."

About the Author

Cynthia Blair, author of books for both adult and young-adult readers, has published more than thirty novels. She grew up on Long Island, New York, and earned her B.A. from Bryn Mawr College. After four years of working in New York City, she began writing full time. She currently lives on Long Island where she, like Miranda, loves spending time outdoors.

☎ 1 (800) I LUV BKS!

If you'd like to hear more about your
favorite young adult novels and writers . . .
OR
If you'd like to tell us what you thought
of this book or other books
you've recently read . . .

CALL US at 1(800) I LUV BKS
[1(800) 458-8257]

You'll hear a new message about books and
other interesting subjects each month.

**The call is free to you, but please get
your parents' permission first.**

▣ HarperPaperbacks *By Mail*

Join KC, Faith, and Winnie as the three hometown friends share the triumphs, loves, and tragedies of their first year of college in this bestselling series:

FRESHMAN DORM

Away from home . . . and on their own!

KC Angeletti: Beautiful and talented, KC is a young woman on the move—and she'll do anything she can to succeed . . .

Winnie Gottlieb: Impulsive, reckless Winnie just can't keep her head on straight—how will she get through her first year?

Faith Crowley: Innocent Faith is Winnie and KC's best friend—but will she ever let loose and be her *own* friend?

Follow all the joys and heartaches of the girls of Freshman Dorm!

"You shouldn't have come," Garth said, his voice even.

"I had to see you," Miranda explained, turning to him.

"You don't belong here."

"Oh, Garth, just hold me!" Disregarding his coldness, she wrapped her arms around him. She desperately needed him to tell her she wasn't alone.

A small eternity passed. And then, finally, he clasped his arms around her fiercely, drawing her close.

It was like coming home.

She raised her face to his. The intensity in his blue eyes created a stirring feeling deep inside. And then he leaned forward, pressing his parted lips against hers. Gently at first, as tentatively as if he were asking a question. But his kiss quickly grew more ardent. Miranda was astonished by the fervor with which she responded. Eagerly she gave in to it. Reaching up, she encircled his neck with her arms, her body melting against his.

Finally he drew back, nuzzling her neck. "My sweet, sweet Miranda," he whispered, his breath hot against her skin.

"Hold me," she pleaded, clinging to him.

He grasped her even more tightly. "Oh, Miranda, what have they done to you?"

Don't miss these exciting books
from HarperPaperbacks!

Dark Moon Legacy
Volume I   *The Curse*
Volume II   *The Seduction*
Volume III   *The Rebellion*

Read these other terrifying thrillers

Sweetheart
Running Scared
by Kate Daniel

Dead Girls Can't Scream
by Janice Harrell

Deadly Stranger
by M. C. Sumner

ATTENTION: ORGANIZATIONS AND CORPORATIONS

Most HarperPaperbacks are available at special quantity
discounts for bulk purchases for sales promotions, premiums,
or fund-raising. For information, please call or write:
**Special Markets Department, HarperCollins Publishers,
10 East 53rd Street, New York, N.Y. 10022
Telephone: (212) 207-7528. Fax (212) 207-7222.**